GIRL, VANISHED

(An Ella Dark FBI Suspense Thriller —Book Five)

BLAKE PIERCE

Blake Pierce

Blake Pierce is the USA Today bestselling author of the RILEY PAGE mystery series, which includes seventeen books. Blake Pierce is also the author of the MACKENZIE WHITE mystery series, comprising fourteen books; of the AVERY BLACK mystery series, comprising six books; of the KERI LOCKE mystery series, comprising five books; of the MAKING OF RILEY PAIGE mystery series, comprising six books; of the KATE WISE mystery series, comprising seven books; of the CHLOE FINE psychological suspense mystery, comprising six books; of the JESSE HUNT psychological suspense thriller series, comprising twenty one books; of the AU PAIR psychological suspense thriller series, comprising three books; of the ZOE PRIME mystery series, comprising six books; of the ADELE SHARP mystery series, comprising fifteen books, of the EUROPEAN VOYAGE cozy mystery series, comprising four books; of the new LAURA FROST FBI suspense thriller, comprising six books (and counting); of the new ELLA DARK FBI suspense thriller, comprising eleven books (and counting); of the A YEAR IN EUROPE cozy mystery series, comprising nine books, of the AVA GOLD mystery series, comprising six books (and counting); and of the RACHEL GIFT mystery series, comprising six books (and counting).

An avid reader and lifelong fan of the mystery and thriller genres, Blake loves to hear from you, so please feel free to visit www.blakepierceauthor.com to learn more and stay in touch.

BOOKS BY BLAKE PIERCE

RACHEL GIFT MYSTERY SERIES
HER LAST WISH (Book #1)
HER LAST CHANCE (Book #2)
HER LAST HOPE (Book #3)
HER LAST FEAR (Book #4)
HER LAST CHOICE (Book #5)
HER LAST BREATH (Book #6)

AVA GOLD MYSTERY SERIES
CITY OF PREY (Book #1)
CITY OF FEAR (Book #2)
CITY OF BONES (Book #3)
CITY OF GHOSTS (Book #4)
CITY OF DEATH (Book #5)
CITY OF VICE (Book #6)

A YEAR IN EUROPE
A MURDER IN PARIS (Book #1)
DEATH IN FLORENCE (Book #2)
VENGEANCE IN VIENNA (Book #3)
A FATALITY IN SPAIN (Book #4)

ELLA DARK FBI SUSPENSE THRILLER
GIRL, ALONE (Book #1)
GIRL, TAKEN (Book #2)
GIRL, HUNTED (Book #3)
GIRL, SILENCED (Book #4)
GIRL, VANISHED (Book 5)
GIRL ERASED (Book #6)
GIRL, FORSAKEN (Book #7)
GIRL, TRAPPED (Book #8)
GIRL, EXPENDABLE (Book #9)
GIRL, ESCAPED (Book #10)

GIRL, HIS (Book #11)

LAURA FROST FBI SUSPENSE THRILLER
ALREADY GONE (Book #1)
ALREADY SEEN (Book #2)
ALREADY TRAPPED (Book #3)
ALREADY MISSING (Book #4)
ALREADY DEAD (Book #5)
ALREADY TAKEN (Book #6)

EUROPEAN VOYAGE COZY MYSTERY SERIES
MURDER (AND BAKLAVA) (Book #1)
DEATH (AND APPLE STRUDEL) (Book #2)
CRIME (AND LAGER) (Book #3)
MISFORTUNE (AND GOUDA) (Book #4)
CALAMITY (AND A DANISH) (Book #5)
MAYHEM (AND HERRING) (Book #6)

ADELE SHARP MYSTERY SERIES
LEFT TO DIE (Book #1)
LEFT TO RUN (Book #2)
LEFT TO HIDE (Book #3)
LEFT TO KILL (Book #4)
LEFT TO MURDER (Book #5)
LEFT TO ENVY (Book #6)
LEFT TO LAPSE (Book #7)
LEFT TO VANISH (Book #8)
LEFT TO HUNT (Book #9)
LEFT TO FEAR (Book #10)
LEFT TO PREY (Book #11)
LEFT TO LURE (Book #12)
LEFT TO CRAVE (Book #13)
LEFT TO LOATHE (Book #14)
LEFT TO HARM (Book #15)

THE AU PAIR SERIES
ALMOST GONE (Book#1)
ALMOST LOST (Book #2)
ALMOST DEAD (Book #3)

BEFORE HE NEEDS (Book #5)
BEFORE HE FEELS (Book #6)
BEFORE HE SINS (Book #7)
BEFORE HE HUNTS (Book #8)
BEFORE HE PREYS (Book #9)
BEFORE HE LONGS (Book #10)
BEFORE HE LAPSES (Book #11)
BEFORE HE ENVIES (Book #12)
BEFORE HE STALKS (Book #13)
BEFORE HE HARMS (Book #14)

AVERY BLACK MYSTERY SERIES
CAUSE TO KILL (Book #1)
CAUSE TO RUN (Book #2)
CAUSE TO HIDE (Book #3)
CAUSE TO FEAR (Book #4)
CAUSE TO SAVE (Book #5)
CAUSE TO DREAD (Book #6)

KERI LOCKE MYSTERY SERIES
A TRACE OF DEATH (Book #1)
A TRACE OF MURDER (Book #2)
A TRACE OF VICE (Book #3)
A TRACE OF CRIME (Book #4)
A TRACE OF HOPE (Book #5)

PROLOGUE

Tessa rustled her key in the lock, not really concerned if it woke up poor old Jimmy, even at this ungodly hour. She should have known Jimmy would forget to put the trash out again. She was rapidly getting fed up with his mistakes. How hard was it to remember a simple task? Every Thursday night, wheel the trash out to the curb. That was it. She wasn't exactly asking him to build a temple. While she was working her backside off at the hospital, Jimmy was probably sitting around, *researching antiques,* as he often claimed. Although in the next breath, he was always quick to say that he was winding down until retirement. Make up your damn mind, she wanted to tell him.

Tessa stepped inside her house, deciding to leave the trash uncollected. Maybe that would teach him. Then again, maybe not. After twenty years of marriage, could you still teach an old husband new tricks?

That was a question for another day. Right now, the question was what to do with the single hour she had before sleep beckoned. She kicked off her work shoes, opened the fridge and stared blankly at its contents, not taking a fancy to anything inside. She didn't have the energy to make a sandwich. Was it going to be the classic berries and cheese? Or was that a bad idea? One of the other nurses once told her that cheese before bed gave you nightmares, and she didn't need any more of those.

Forget it. Decaf and trash television was the easiest route. She left the kitchen and walked into the living area, and there she sensed another soul in the room. She instinctively reached for the light switch but stopped herself from turning it on. She saw the silhouette of her beloved husband, passed out in the chair, crumpled blanket lying at his feet. Tessa sighed, realizing that an hour in front of the TV was a no-go. If she woke Jimmy up, he'd be a miserable trout until at least tomorrow afternoon. She didn't need that.

Forget it. May as well hit the hay. Tessa gently opened the living room door, careful not to disturb her snoozing husband, half out of genuine affection and half for the fact she'd get the bed to herself. She left her bag on the couch as a sign of her safe arrival back home. Not

1

only that, but it might persuade Jimmy to spend the night downstairs and give her some peace too.

Tessa hit the bathroom and rubbed off the little makeup she had on. She changed out of her uniform and brushed away the stale taste of twelve hours of giving instructions. Over the sink, she looked out of the window and admired the night. There was something about returning home in the early hours of the morning that really played havoc with the senses. While everyone else slept, you were on the front lines, keeping the world moving. It was enough to give weaker minds a hero complex.

She sat down on the toilet as she re-applied her ponytail but stopped as she reached the third and final knot.

A noise. Some kind of scratching. Or a rustling? It seemed to come from behind.

Tessa jerked her head towards the windowsill and took a step back out of fear of what she might find. She glanced between the gaps in her lotion bottles, then found the culprit. A small box that once housed moisturizer had tipped over. When she reached out to grab it, she felt the draft from the window gap graze her fingertips.

Jimmy had left the window ajar, again. She was sick of telling him about that. The breeze must have knocked the empty box over, and why was there an empty box here anyway? She couldn't blame her husband for that. That was her doing.

She pulled the window shut, sat down and returned to her pre-sleep ritual. She got the ponytail back in and then searched for the anti-wrinkle cream.

But before she landed on it, the noise came again. Scratching, or crunching. It was difficult to place. Could it be the water rushing through the pipes? Maybe the toilet was acting up again? Suddenly, she jerked her hand back when the sound seemed to emerge right from her fingertips.

Tessa rushed back to the door in panic. The noise became louder, more frantic. She didn't know what it was, but she was certain it was the sound of something alive.

Then, like a ghoul rising from the depths of hell, the source of the noise made itself known.

A black smudge, fluttering and flapping, rose from between her lotion bottles and flung itself towards the bathroom light.

"Agh, Jesus Christ," Tessa yelled as she retreated out into the hallway. She peered through a gap, unable to take her eyes off the thing. Like a miniature dragon, the creature beat its wings furiously

2

while it clashed with the glaring light: a battle that would only yield one winner. But it didn't stop the beast from trying.

What was it? A moth? One of those giant moths that had emigrated from down under and settled in Delaware of all places? Whatever it was, it looked like an omen of death. Big, furry, black as charcoal. Tessa pulled the door shut, trapping the beast inside her small bathroom. Those things made her feel queasy, and if the creature had to die so she could sleep, so be it.

She had to laugh. She'd shut the window. If she'd have left it open, the thing might have had an escape route. Now it was her unwanted prisoner, and there was no way she was heading back in to face it.

This was a Jimmy situation, she decided. He was the designated insect-killer in the house. That had been established from day one. Tessa headed back downstairs with heavy footsteps, hoping it would jolt Jimmy awake before she got there.

It didn't. The living room was still darkened but she made out Jimmy's form sprawled in the same position as before.

"Jim," she said, slightly above a whisper. "Jimmy. Wake up."

Nothing.

"Hey, Jim. We have a problem."

Nope. Dead to the world. Time to go nuclear.

Tessa moved over to him and fondled his leg. He was cold, almost icy. She shook him again. "Jim, get up. I need you."

There was no muscle response, no reaction from his nerve endings. How could he sleep so deeply when she could be woken up by a cooing pigeon? Some people get all the luck.

"Jimmy," she said, louder this time. She squeezed his leg a little harder, digging in a portion of fingernail.

Not a thing.

Tessa felt the air leave her lungs. Her brow began to burn with sweat. This wasn't normal, even for Jimmy.

She grabbed his hand. Cold as winter frost. She shook him, enough to jerk anyone back to consciousness. There was nothing. Tessa grabbed Jimmy's face with both hands, feeling cold flesh, rough skin and, to her dread, something wet.

In the gloom, she saw something in Jimmy's eyes. They looked shut, but there was a shine emanating from them, as though they were both tunnels leading directly to the afterlife.

Her vision adjusted to the darkness in panic. Tessa jumped to her feet, her first thought being that she had thirty years of medical training

3

to draw on. Her husband was fit and healthy. He had plenty more years left in him. This couldn't be happening.

Tessa rushed over to the wall and searched for the light switch with trembling hands. She found it, but her fingers wouldn't let herself push it. Doing so would bring this horror to life, and something told her it was a moment she'd remember for the rest of her days regardless of how it played out.

Light cast the room in bright yellow.

Tessa's hands shot to her mouth but did nothing to stop her screams.

All her energy left her body and she felt to her knees in hopelessness. This was nothing her medical training could fix. No one could fix this. Even the most masterful surgeon would consider this a lost cause on sight.

Jimmy sat slumped in his chair, dried blood coating his neck and t-shirt. He was a lifeless specimen, something Tessa had seen plenty of in her time, but never once did she think the body would belong to the man she loved.

A second wave of despair came when she realized she'd walked right past him only a few minutes ago. She scrambled around for her phone to call the police, but before her jittering hands could dial the number, she saw something that seemed out of place, even for a morbid scene like this.

She saw a sign of life in her husband.

In her frenzy, she hadn't seen it right away. She had been too engulfed with panic. She reluctantly shuffled closer, wiping away the tears with her forearm as she did.

Then came a third wave of despair when she realized it wasn't a sign of life at all. Jimmy's eyes reflected beams of golden light, as though death had transformed them into tiny mirrors.

On closer scrutiny, it had.

Because Jimmy now had silver coins where his eyes should have been.

Tessa lost all basic functions: voice, mobility, cognitive thought. She managed to dial the emergency service number, and when it connected, all she could do was scream on the line.

CHAPTER ONE

Ella Dark sat on her apartment floor, paperwork piled high on every side. She checked her phone.

One message from Mark.

I'll pick you up in 10 mins, followed by a row of XX's.

Ella checked the time. Seven-thirty AM. She'd woken up two hours earlier after a bizarre dream in which she was singing to a packed audience with an orchestra; only when she turned around, the musicians had no faces. She hoped it was just her imagination taking liberties rather than a metaphorical manifestation of her thoughts.

She was ready to go; but before she left, she had to make a dent in this paperwork.

Two weeks ago, she'd apprehended the sex worker killer down in Baltimore after a grueling battle. She'd been the one to physically take him down, but it had been a team effort between her, Agent Mia Ripley and Agent Mark Balzano to get the circumstances right.

The wounds were beginning to heal, at least the physical ones. She'd suffered a few injuries, but the FBI doctors had set her right. However, the mental wounds were still an inescapable abyss that seemed to widen by the day.

Agent Ripley had discovered Ella's deceit. Ella had been conversing with incarcerated serial killer Tobias Campbell, something that she'd gone to great lengths to keep from her partner given Ripley's history with him. Ripley had been the one to take Campbell down fifteen years earlier, but it wasn't without its traumas. Ella had kept her partner in the dark out of concern for her reaction, and Ripley had reacted exactly as Ella expected when she finally found out. Worse, in fact.

But while Ella still called Ripley her partner in her own thoughts, the more appropriate term was ex-partner. Ripley told Ella they couldn't be a team anymore. Ripley's last words to Ella before she stormed off was that she was putting in a request for a new trainee.

So far, Ella didn't know if Ripley had made good on her claim. She hadn't seen or talked to her in two weeks, although it wasn't for Ella's lack of trying. She'd sent texts, made calls, and tried to catch her at FBI HQ to no avail.

Ella wanted nothing more than to apologize, even though words really couldn't convey just how much of a fool she felt. Her career in the field might have come to a close, and while she hated that fact, it was what she deserved. Not only did she go behind her partner's back, the same woman who'd saved her life multiple times over the past six months, but it was laughable to think she could meet with one of the country's most notorious criminals and keep it secret. It had been Campbell himself who'd divulged the details to Ripley. He'd sent her a letter, explaining everything in full. She had opened herself up to a human predator and he'd reacted exactly as one might expect. It was no one's fault but her own.

And it wasn't just Campbell's written acknowledgments that haunted her day and night. It was Campbell himself, at least through proxy. Campbell was a spider at the center of a giant web, and he had contacts all across the country and possibly further. His disciples had eyes on her, watching her every movement and leaving dead animals on her doorstep. Every time Ella left the house, she was dreadfully wary of anyone who passed her, any stranger who made idle conversation, any leaflet distributor who shamelessly invaded her space. Any one of them could be a Campbell disciple, and one day, one of them would be.

Her last cause of concern regarded that of her deceased father. Twenty-five years ago, she'd found her old man dead in his bed and the perpetrator had never been uncovered. Two weeks ago, she'd tracked down a man named Richie Cunningham, who sources told her was an old foe of her dad's. Richie denied any involvement in her dad's murder but told Ella that her dad had some serious money issues. He owed the wrong people, allegedly. It was the first Ella heard of such a thing, but she was going to dig deeper regardless. The piles of paperwork that lay beside her were her father's possessions. Bills, receipts, letters. If there was something here that scratched the surface of the truth, she'd find it.

But concentration didn't come easy, not with the smorgasbord of troubles weighing her down. It was getting late now, but she still had the paperwork from 1993 to 1995 to go through. She took a few shots of whiskey and lime to keep the tiredness at bay, a trick her ex-partner taught her. The lime to boost concentration levels, and the whiskey because it was whiskey. She picked up the next pile and leafed through it for any discriminate documents, something that didn't follow the usual format of soulless greeting, request for money, informal signoff. The edges of the paper became a blur as her tiredness took over, but then the bottom half of the stack fell from her hands. Ella glanced at the yellowed piece of paper laying on the top of the pile.

A different size from the rest. Not standard paper size, or a standard letterhead.

And it was entirely handwritten.

Some of the ink had faded with time, but the content was mostly legible.

Ken, consider this your acknowledgment of borrowed monies. Must be repaid in full, with ten percent interest by 05/25/95. OWA.

Ella almost dropped the rest of the paperwork when she saw the date.

Five days before her father had been killed.

Her hands trembled as she reached out for it, but then her detective instincts kicked in. She gently picked it up by its corner, held it and scrutinized every inch of it. Written in black ink, only a few sentences on the front and nothing on the back. If this had been left among this paperwork for two decades, there was a chance the creator's fingerprints were still on it somewhere.

But what was this anyway?

Some kind of receipt? And a handwritten one at that? No reputable establishment would use such irregular paper, so was this some kind of backdoor transaction? And why was there no mention of the actual amount?

Ella quickly flicked through the rest of the paperwork to see if she could find any similar documents. None. Nothing that resembled this one. It was a one-off.

Something wasn't right about this. And the biggest question was – who was *OWA*? Someone's initials? The name of an organization? She had some digging to do. She put the document in a plastic wallet to keep it safe then stashed it away.

It was Monday now, and that meant it was back to life in the office, back to the world of Intelligence. But any second that she had to spare, she planned on hunting down Mia and spilling her apologies out. It had been two weeks now, and surely Mia couldn't stay mad at her forever.

Ella's phone pinged again.

Outside! x

Ella hurried to the door, leaving behind her stacks of files. Since they'd met, she'd taken a real liking to Mark Balzano. One date turned into two, and two turned into a casual relationship. Now, she wasn't desperate to make things official, at least not yet, because such things came with time. She wasn't one for jumping into relationships, especially with someone she worked with, although such circumstances were a new venture to her.

Outside her complex, spring was in full sway, but the pleasant temperatures and moderate sunlight did very little to quench her worries. Mark's sedan was waiting right at the door. Ella jumped in and greeted Mark with a kiss on the lips.

"You're early," she said. "Punctuality is a very attractive quality in a man."

"Five minutes ahead of schedule. Right on schedule," Mark said.

Mark was a seasoned agent but was currently sidelined due to an injury. He'd been assigned to administrative work for the time being, although it didn't stop him from helping Ella out in the field when she needed it last time. He had his FBI-issue jacket on today, and he'd tied his hair back in a stumpy ponytail. It was a bold move, but he got away with it.

"How are you holding up?" he asked. "Did you find anything in your dad's stuff?"

She liked Mark because he understood her. They had the same approaches and philosophies when it came to saving lives and exacting justice, and it didn't hurt that he had a chiseled jawline she could admire for hours.

There was just one thing that concerned her.

They drove out on the main road towards the freeway. FBI HQ was a forty-five-minute venture, double in rush hour.

"A lot of it was useless, but I did find one thing. Some kind of receipt."

"A receipt? For what?"

"I don't know exactly," Ella said. "It was handwritten and just mentioned *borrowed monies*."

Mark turned the radio dial down. "That could be anything. It could be a friend of his just being anal after lending him ten dollars. Or it could be a joke."

Ella considered it. "I suppose. But why would he keep it?"

"Sentimental reasons? I don't know. I'm just guessing. But it's definitely worth checking out."

"Absolutely. I'm going to try it for prints first. If nothing comes back, then I'll try matching the handwriting. Then if there's still nothing…"

8

Mark slammed the brakes on as another vehicle swerved in front of them. Ella clutched the armrest as the car abruptly slowed to a crawl.

She braced herself, predicting backlash on Mark's part.

"Damn. Close one," he said.

Ella waited a second for the moment to pass. If there was one thing about Mark that she didn't quite *get,* it was his temper. On their first date, Mark had berated a restaurant customer for almost knocking his drink over. A minor inconvenience, but one Mark blew up to extravagant proportions. Ella brushed it off as a one-off and Mark apologized profusely, but since then, she was on alert around him. In the past two weeks, he'd been fine, but the worry was still there.

"Monday drivers," Ella said. "Typical."

"Rushing to work to sit in a cubicle for eight hours."

Ella shrugged. "Maybe. He might be a doctor or something though."

"Doubt it. It was a woman."

Ella scratched her head. Some lame attempt at humor? "That's a bit..."

"Joke," Mark interrupted. "I'm kidding. Just trying to lighten the mood. I'm a bit worried about you. What with all your recent troubles."

Ella sped through a series of responses, landing on frustration. It was too early for this. "I'm fine. I just need time to process everything, but I appreciate the concern."

They moved got onto the freeway. It looked clear for a few miles but no doubt the traffic would creep in closer to the city.

"What are you gonna be doing from now on?" Mark asked. "You're still working out in the field occasionally, right?"

"Same thing as the last two weeks. Working in Intelligence until the director calls on me. *If* he calls on me. He hasn't said a word to me since Ripley ditched me. I'm starting to think my special agent days are behind me."

"Retired in what, less than a year? You lasted longer than some people."

Ella stared out at the passing buildings. Familiar sights she'd seen a thousand times, but they brought her an indescribable comfort.

"I want to do it a lot longer. Working behind a desk just isn't the same as actually being out there."

Mark rolled down his window and rested his elbow in the gap, the other hand on the wheel. "Tell me about it. You actually feel like you're making a difference when you're in the thick of it, don't you?"

"One hundred percent," Ella sighed. "Now I just feel like I'm waiting. Waiting for bad news, or something worse. It sucks."

"If you want to help me out, I can make a request. You get to be a little closer to the action but still keep your distance. Like window shopping."

Ella thought about it for a second but didn't like the idea. She was better off where she knew she had a job.

"Thanks for the offer but I don't think it would work. At least I know what I'm doing in Intelligence. Well, I think I do. It's all been a bit of a blur recently."

"Don't sweat it. Things will work out." Mark reached over and rubbed her thigh. "The director's a busy man. He's got governors on his ass, politicians, government big wigs. You think he's got time for a nobody like you?"

Ella glanced at Mark. Her narrowed eyes met his. He smiled.

"Kidding. Come on. You know what I mean."

She shook her head and laughed. "With a sense of humor like that, you're wasted at the bureau."

Mark nodded. "You think I'd make a good standup?"

Ella's phone buzzed in her pocket. She pulled it out. "I was thinking more funeral director." She stared at the notification, suddenly transported to a different plane of existence. Her heart stopped for a second.

Mark caught wind of her change. "Problem?" he asked.

She heard his words but didn't register them. The thoughts came thick and fast, and she had to roll down the window so the fresh air could cleanse them.

"Turns out he's not too busy for a nobody like me."

"The director wants you?"

Ella read the message aloud.

Come to my office immediately. We need to have a discussion.

CHAPTER TWO

Inside the FBI offices, Ella stood outside Director William Edis's office. She could see his blurred outline behind the frosted glass, hunched over his desk in a pose of professionalism that induced new dread in her. She knocked with a trembling hand.

By now, Edis would have had time to ruminate on recent events. Mia would have told Edis everything, out of both spite and professional courtesy. Edis must know about Ella's meetings with Tobias Campbell, but it was only a month ago that Edis gave Ella the choice to see Campbell or not. She'd done it, but the crime was that she didn't inform the higher-ups. She also spilled details of ongoing investigations to the killer, and Edis would no doubt have something to say about that.

"Come in," Edis bellowed from behind the door.

Ella opened slowly and entered. "Morning, Mr. Edis."

"Miss Dark. Please sit down."

He looked like he'd lost a few pounds since she last saw him. His stocky frame still obscured most of the window behind his desk, but there was new shape to his usually circular face. The rumor around HQ was that he was going through a divorce so maybe this was a side-effect. He pushed his glasses up with one finger and motioned to the leather chair against the wall.

Ella took a seat. Her heart raced like a trapped bird in her chest, and she wondered whether this might be the last time she ever saw the interior of this office. Maybe this would be her last day at the FBI. A seven-year career, from Intelligence Analyst to Special Agent to disgraced ex-employee. A common career path but not one she ever envisioned for herself.

She tried her best to stay calm. She kept her feet flat on the ground and controlled her breathing. She had an answer for everything; God knows she'd rehearsed her lines enough over the past two weeks.

Edis sat back in his chair and looked up to the ceiling. He took a deep breath. Ella braced herself.

"I'm sure you know what this is about," Edis said.

Ella nodded. She clasped her hands beneath her chin. "Yes, I do, sir."

"Agent Ripley has informed me of everything. *Everything*. So, I'm not sure how to put this."

"Please, sir, I can handle it. I know I made a big mistake. I'm ready to deal with the consequences."

The director cracked his knuckles then tilted his head to one side. "What you did was foolish and irresponsible. Agent Ripley had every right to suspend your working relationship."

"I understand why she did it," said Ella, somehow holding herself together. This felt like the lead-up to a final crushing blow. Ella grabbed her leg to stop it twitching. She wished Edis would just get it over and done with.

"But it should be said that Agent Ripley and I regularly have a difference of opinion. Personally, I don't blame you for what you did."

The dread numbed a little. Ella wasn't sure she was hearing him right. "Excuse me? Really?" she asked.

William Edis blew a gust of air out of his nose. "You had an opportunity; you took it. Yes, I wish you would have been a little more transparent about things. I know it was a personal invitation from Campbell, but given his history with Agent Ripley, I think you had a duty to keep her informed. You had a moral duty, but no legal duty, so it's a tricky one for me."

"Sir, I understand, but the reason I didn't tell Agent Ripley is because I didn't want to hurt her. I thought I would meet Campbell, learn a few things from him and part ways. Nothing more. I didn't know the extent it would go."

"I get it, Miss Dark. You're young and hungry, desperate to make a difference. I was young and hungry once too, before paperwork and politics got the better of me. If this was thirty years ago and I was in your shoes, I'd have done the same thing. I might have told my partner, but I'd have done the same thing."

The abyss beneath her grew smaller. Ella was suddenly overwhelmed with relief.

"Oh, well, I must say I didn't expect that response. Thank you for having mercy," she said.

"You're most welcome, but there's still the matter of you divulging vital information about an ongoing investigation to Mr. Campbell. Now that, I do have an issue with."

She wasn't out of the woods yet, she thought. But her punishment was deserved, and she was ready to take it.

"You're absolutely right, sir. I shouldn't have done that. It was reckless and unprofessional. Campbell seemed to have all the answers and I was desperate. But I'm not here to make excuses."

Edis picked up a brown folder and leafed through it. The sticker on the front declared it was the folder for an active case.

"The good news is that since that case is now solved, the information Tobias has isn't really an issue. But under other circumstances, this would be a disciplinary, maybe even a suspension without pay. Do I make myself clear? No more secret rendezvous with Campbell and no more divulging confidential details. Understand?"

"Crystal clear, sir," Ella said. "I assure you it won't happen again."

"Good. Now, with that said, I can't speak for Agent Ripley. Like I said, she and I have our differences of opinion, and this is one of them, which is why I've assigned you a new partner."

Ella involuntarily stood up. The frustration burned her limbs. "What? She actually went through with it?"

Edis held up his palms. "Please Miss Dark, sit down. This isn't a time for overreactions."

Ella forcefully rubbed her temples. "I can't believe that. I thought she was just bluffing. After everything she and I have been through, all the times she didn't believe my theories when I was right all along, and she ditches me?"

In the back of her mind, Ella expected Mia to request a new partner, but the reality of it actually happening stirred up a new level of grief.

"She requested it, Ella. There was nothing I could do."

This was it. Her career in the field coming to an abrupt end. She felt like she was on a treadmill chasing a never-ending finish line.

"I have to call her," Ella shouted. She pulled her phone out and dialed Mia's cell phone. Her call history already showed 16 calls to Mia in the past two weeks, all of which went unanswered. Something told her that this one, under the bright lights of working hours, might prompt her to pick up. She burst out back into the foyer leaving Edis alone, foregoing all professionalism in the process. Emotion drove her. She listened to the dial tone. Two, three, four rings.

With the phone pressed to her ear, she scanned the area, hoping that by some miracle Mia might appear. There were faces she recognized, but no sign of her ex-partner.

The line cut out.

Not voicemail. Her call had been rejected.

"Hello?" said a voice. "Ella Dark?"

Ella spun around to find a man staring at her. Shaved head, slightly taller than her. He was wearing a gray suit with a red tie. He had deep brown eyes, sharp cheekbones, and a skinny physique.

She pocketed her phone. "Yes? That's me."

The man reached out his hand. "Agent Byford. Good to finally meet you."

Ella retraced the last few minutes. Had she missed something? She'd never seen this man or heard his name before. She returned the gesture with a confused look.

"Ella Dark. What do you mean, finally meet me?"

Agent Byford passed his briefcase between his hands. "You haven't been told?"

The door behind them opened and Edis stuck his head out. Ella turned to him.

"Miss Dark," Edis said, "this is Agent Nigel Byford. He's your new partner."

"Huh?" Ella said, startled. "New partner?"

"Yes, now come back inside. You have a new case to worry about."

Ella glanced between Edis and this new agent. It all felt like a fever dream.

***

Ella sat on one side of the office; Byford sat on the other. She eyed him up and down without making it too obvious. Was she expected to just hit the road with this stranger? At least she knew who Mia Ripley was beforehand, but she'd never heard of a Nigel Byford in her whole career. Maybe he was new, or was she here to train *him*?

"Agent Byford," said Edis, "I'm sure you've seen Miss Dark around. You've probably heard her name by now."

Byford looked up from his notepad. "Yes, I have. It's a pleasure to meet you." His voice had a California twang. Soft-spoken but firm.

"She's four cases in, four cases down, so she's on a good trajectory. Under your wing, we're hoping we can keep it going."

"I'll do everything I can, sir."

It looked like she was still the trainee. It stung a little.

"Miss Dark, Agent Byford is another of our seasoned field veterans. He's been with us longer than I can remember."

"Fifteen years, sir. Hoping for fifteen more."

Ella had to wonder why she'd never heard his name before. She decided she'd get to that when she had time to chat.

"Good. Well, what we've got here is something very strange," Edis said. "Newark, Delaware. We've got two dead bodies. The first was killed three nights ago, the second one last night. Local police have called us in due to the, shall we say, bizarre nature of the crimes."

Edis threw a brown folder to each of the agents. Ella opened it and scanned the pages. The first thing that drew her attention was the graphic crime scene photos of the first victim. The first picture showed a middle-aged man dead in his chair, throat slashed, blood dousing his torso. The next photo was a close-up of his face.

"Oh my God. Are those…coins?" Ella asked.

"Yes, they are," Edis said. "Our unsub seems to have a very unique signature."

Ella thought about it. If Mia was here, she'd say that placing coins in the eyes was part of the ritual, not the signature. Ella let it slide. She scanned her memory bank for historical serial killers who'd focused on the eyes and came up with two names. She did the same for coins and found nothing."

"Interesting," said Byford. "The coins might be symbolic."

Ella let the moment hang in the air. Such a comment needed elaboration, surely. None came.

Yeah, you reckon? she thought.

"Both men were killed in their homes, and both were of similar age. The unsub slashed their throats then placed coins in their eyes, postmortem. Local teams are securing the second crime scene as we speak. They're also waiting on forensic reports from the first one. Dark, Byford, any ideas?"

"None as of yet," Byford jumped in. "I just need some time to organize my thoughts. There's a lot to take in."

Ella had plenty of ideas but didn't want to blurt them all out straight away. But she also wanted to improve her graces with Edis given their recent troubles. "These coins could represent a number of things, but I'm more concerned with the killing method."

Byford looked up from his file. "Why's that?"

"A single slash to the throat and no other lacerations. It suggests he can blitz attack his victims with precision or subdue them without force. It means he's skilled, cunning, and able to invade homes without being detected He isn't just some run-of-the-mill sociopath. We're dealing with a capable, organized psychopath hell-bent on sending some kind of twisted message."

Byford nodded. "I can see we're going to have a lot to talk about."

What did that mean? Ella hadn't taken a liking to this new guy. She never believed the old adage about first impressions, but she was starting to.

"We are indeed," she said.

"I need you both out there pronto," said Edis. "Admin have already arranged your flights and motels. When you get there, I want you to meet with the local PD and they'll fill you in. A crime like this is going to stir up a lot of fear. That means the press are going to come down hard on us, and it's me who answers their questions. I don't need to tell you that we need this perpetrator caught yesterday."

"Understood, sir," Byford said. "I'm on it." He turned to Ella. "Should we convene at the airport?"

Ella nodded. "Alright. See you there."

This guy wasn't giving her much to work with. Should they meet on the plane? In the lounge? She didn't question it. This was her case to solve, she thought. Her chance to show she could do this on her own.

Byford made his way to the door. Ella collected her bag and followed.

"Miss Dark, could you stay behind for a moment?" Edis asked.

Ella reluctantly turned around. "Of course, sir." She nodded goodbye to her new partner and shut the door, feeling a little rude doing so. "What is it you need?"

He ushered her back towards his desk then perched himself on it. "Nigel Byford is a very good agent. He's what I call a field general, so you'll be in safe hands when it comes to procedures and legalities."

"I have no doubt. He seems very level-headed."

"Very much so. But he's originally from counterterrorism. He can negotiate his way out of life and death situations like no one else, but he doesn't have the…" Edis searched for the word. "Insight? That you might have."

"I see," Ella said. Was Edis prepping her for something? This seemed a strange conversation to have. "So he's not a behavioral expert?"

"Not in regard to the extreme psychopathic or psychotic minds. He understands twisted fundamentalist minds better than anyone on our books, but domestic serial killers are a relatively new avenue for him."

"I understand. So, should I guide him as much as he guides me? Is that what you mean?"

"A little. You also don't need reminding that this is your first case without Ripley by your side. If you come back victorious, who's to say what that might do for you?"

The thought had already crossed Ella's mind. Her previous cases all had Mia's name attached to them, so she was the focal point, she was the star. If Ella solved this without Mia's involvement, that could put her on the same level. Not to mention, it could prompt Mia to contact her again. Maybe earn some of Mia's respect back in the process.

"I'm on it, sir. I'll do everything I can to bring this case home. You have my word."

Ella grabbed her bag and headed straight to the airport. She was back in the game, and nothing felt better.

CHAPTER THREE

Mia Ripley stood inside the top floor apartment in Manhattan. The body of a young man lay on a plush gray sofa, two gaping holes in either side of his skull. Some forensic technicians swabbed the area while Mia took in her surroundings.

Such a lovely building, home to retired bankers and young professionals mostly. But in places like this, or any lavish apartment complex in any major city, there was always a consistency: suicide. Mia walked around the one-floor home, admiring the décor, scrutinizing the contents left behind. On a coffee table in front of the man sat a remote control. Beside that was a glass of water, and next to that was a fishing magazine.

Lodged in the man's right hand was a .22 caliber pistol.

Mia moved back to the lounge where the technicians were finishing up. She put her hands on her hips and sighed. "Thoughts?" she asked.

"City boys and suicide. Name a more iconic duo," Melissa said.

So far, Melissa Santos hadn't offered much in the way of ideas. The entire plane ride here she'd been mostly silent, staring at her phone for a good portion of the journey. Now, she seemed to dismiss the scene with a simple assumption.

"Do you think?"

"For sure. Look at the arrangements. He has bullet holes on either side of his head. This guy was probably a Wall Street executive struggling with the financial collapse. This was his way out."

Mia looked back towards the kitchen at a half-buttered knife sitting on the surface. She walked over to it, examined it, then checked the fridge and cupboard contents. Alcohol bottles, mostly expensive rums lined the shelves. Chocolate, sugary goods everywhere. On the kitchen surface was a 200-pack of cigarettes. Mia returned to the lounge and instinctively looked towards the plug sockets around the room, and after spotting two, her suspicions were confirmed.

"Tell me why this was a suicide," Mia said to Melissa. "I mean, it looks pretty open and shut, but we need to back it up with evidence.

More importantly, tell me why this was the third Manhattan suicide in the span a week."

Suicide wasn't contagious and in the rare cases it seemed to be, there was always something else afoot. If it was a standalone suicide, there'd be no need for FBI intervention. This was the first clue Mia was trying to sneak into her new partner.

Melissa was a new recruit, plucked from the FBI's Cyber Security division. She was 25 years old, tall, blonde and in Mia's opinion, dressed like a librarian. She'd shown promise, and an interest in moving into field work, so Ripley handpicked her to accompany on this new case.

Only a few hours in, Mia was already regretting it.

"There's a gun in his hand," Melissa said. "Bullet holes in his head. He's obviously single judging by this apartment. Plus, this guy was a junkie. There's some white powder on the table which I'm guessing is cocaine. Plus, joint ends in an ashtray."

"So he liked drugs," Mia said.

"He got high to build up the courage then pulled the trigger. Bang, " Melissa poised her fingertips like a gun and clicked her thumb. Mia thought it was a bit distasteful, especially for a newbie.

Mia pulled out her phone to snap a picture of the victim. On her home screen she saw another missed call from Ella. Did that woman not get the message? By now, Ella would have learned of Mia's new partner, and it would have kicked Ella right in the gut. Not her problem.

Mia had no time for sympathy, not considering everything Ella had done. She brought this whole situation on herself and for that, Mia couldn't apologize or empathize. Consequences had actions and Ella had to learn that the hard way.

For a moment, Mia wondered how Ella might view this scene. Would she have an outlandish theory? Would she label it a suicide too? Or would she look at the clues, at the *evidence*, and come to the same conclusion Mia had?

Mia guessed the latter, but even so, Ella was gone from her life and wasn't going to be invited back. Mia had molded Ella into a competent agent, and it had taken considerable time and considerable hardships. She couldn't expect Melissa to be on the same level on her first day.

But she just wished that Melissa had a little more awareness. Maybe it was a young person thing. Entitlement came first, hard work second. Or was she just being presumptuous? Mia cleared her thoughts and focused on the task at hand. She wasn't going to tell Melissa what to look for but decided to prompt her in that direction.

"Put yourself in this man's shoes," Mia said. "What was he thinking when he did it? Why did he do it here? Why now? Is there anything missing from this picture that doesn't make sense? Put the pieces together and see what comes up. You might be surprised."

Melissa furiously typed something on her phone. Mia glanced over and saw she was texting someone. Melissa pocketed it and glanced around the room again, looking a little lost this time.

"Stress?" Melissa asked.

"Of what? This guy seems to have done pretty well for himself. He's young, good looking and successful. What's he got to be stressed about?"

Melissa bent down and inspected the contents of the table. Magazine, water, TV remote. It was a perfect scene. A little too perfect. She held up her hands in defeat. "Sorry, I'm not seeing anything out of the ordinary."

Mia tried not to audibly sigh. "Have you ever heard the term staging?" she asked.

"Of course. Why?"

"What does it mean?"

Melissa looked confused. "Setting the scene. Making something look good. Like a show home."

Mia waited for the lightbulb to go off in her new partner's head. She'd just said the exact words she was looking for. Silence took over and they were back to square one.

"Santos, the facts are right in front of us. There are at least four pieces of evidence here that show what really happened. Look more closely at this picture. There are juxtapositions here that stand out. It's our job to find them."

Was she being too hard on her? Mia thought back to her first case with Ella when she'd seen the truth immediately. The Ed Gein copycat. She remembered Ella finding that skinned face in the bottom of a barrel where no one else thought to look.

Melissa sauntered around the apartment, perhaps more for effect than genuine investigation. Mia saw right through it. She gave her points for trying.

"I'm sorry, partner, I'm not seeing it," Melissa said without an ounce of concern. "It all looks cut and dry to me."

"Okay, I'll tell you what to look at. The butter knife in the kitchen, the plug sockets in the walls and the bullet wounds in this guy's head. Look at them. One of these things isn't like the others."

Melissa moved back and forth between the things she mentioned. Her movements reminded her of one of those robot vacuums that did a sudden 360 when it hit a wall. *Give her time,* Mia thought. *You can't pick this job up in a day.*

Mia moved over to the giant window at the apartment's far end. It offered an incredible view of the city, almost anxiety-inducing given the sheer height they were at. Below, people and cars moved around like ants. To her, New York was only one rung below California in terms of places she didn't want to be. She glanced back to find Melissa running her bare fingers around the victim's bullet wounds.

"Santos. Be careful. Put your gloves on before doing that."

"I barely touched it. Don't worry."

Mia dismissed the comment. "Any thoughts yet?"

"Am I supposed to be seeing something other than the obvious? Because I'm struggling here."

Mia decided to just explain it all in full. Melissa clearly wasn't going to figure it out. She moved over to the victim and pointed to his right temple. "You see this hole? It's bigger than the hole on the left side. What does that mean?"

"That the bullet entered on the right side?" Melissa said with a smile.

"Yes. The bullet entered in the right and exited on the left. What does that tell you about our man?"

"Umm," Melissa stumbled. "That he shot himself in the head?" She said it with a lighthearted tone that Mia didn't appreciate.

"No, it suggests our victim was right-handed. You ever held a gun before?"

Melissa's eyes glanced towards the ceiling. "A few times."

"And what hand do you pull the trigger with? Your dominant hand, yes?"

"Yeah, my right."

"Yes, because pulling the trigger requires a good amount of force, not to mention it's easier to aim and control with your dominant hand. Now, look around this apartment. What do you see?"

"Just... normal stuff," Melissa shrugged. "TV, table, clock. What am I looking for?"

Mia pointed to the two wall sockets. "Only the left-hand sockets have been used." She motioned for Melissa to join her in the kitchen. "See this knife? It has butter on the right-hand side of it, meaning our guy swipes from the left. He isn't right-handed; he's left-handed."

It took Melissa a moment to connect the dots. "Woah, wait a second. You mean these two little things prove he was left-handed? What if it's a coincidence? Or what if someone else buttered this knife?"

"No, there are other things too. Look at the layout of the room. People naturally put their important possessions on their dominant side. Righties put their TVs and furniture on the right side of the room, lefties the opposite. This entire place is a leftie's apartment. And now, look at the things on the table in front of our guy. Magazine, water, both placed to his right. Bullet wound on the right. No left-handed person is gonna shoot with their right. It's not natural."

Melissa looked like she'd just been told the secrets of the universe. "Oh, wowza. That's incredible. So, you're saying he didn't kill himself?"

Mia was happy Melissa finally put the pieces together but frustrated it took longer than a few minutes. "No, this whole scene has been staged. Plus there's the matter of the drugs. That's sativa weed he's smoking judging by the smell. Sativa and cocaine are the busy man's drugs. They help with focus and concentration. If he was going to off himself, he'd take something to sedate him. There's plenty of alcohol to choose from and he didn't."

Melissa's face flushed white, like she'd just heard a story and completely missed the take-home message. Mia saw a touch of embarrassment and suddenly wondered if she wasn't coming across condescending. Back in the day, she wouldn't care about such things, but the rookie had made her more self-aware when dealing with non-professionals.

"Damn. I can't believe I didn't see that. I didn't even consider it. You think this was a murder?"

"I have no doubt," Mia said. "Water and a fishing magazine? This guy lives on drugs and sugar, and there are no fishing hotspots around here for miles. This guy had enemies and we need to find out who."

Melissa stood in place, taking it all in. But even so, Mia couldn't really see the cogs whirring in her mind. If this was Ella, she'd already have a theory and be desperate to get back to base. Melissa looked like a kid lost in the fog. Mia put her hand on her arm.

"It's alright if you didn't see it right away. Learning these things takes time, and that's why I'm here with you, alright?"

Melissa thanked her, made a few notes, then continued looking around the apartment. If there was one thing Mia was certain of, it was that this new partner wouldn't take any chances any time soon. She wouldn't keep her in the dark. Mia had learned to read people in record time over her thirty years in the game, and Melissa Santos wasn't the type to take risks, nor was she type to visit an old nemesis behind Mia's back.

No, very few people had the balls to do that.

CHAPTER FOUR

Ella and Byford sat in the back of the cab together en route to the fresh crime scene. They'd been seated in standard class on the flight there and they hadn't even been seated together. It must have been a perk of Mia's notoriety that allowed them business class on their previous flights.

He seemed like a decent enough man but appeared a little closed off to her. His head was always down, hidden in his laptop or his casefile. He said they would have a lot to talk about but hadn't made any effort so far.

"Nigel, I hear you're from counter-terrorism?" Ella asked.

Byford didn't look up. He typed away on his laptop. "I am. I spent over ten years there. Where are you from?"

"I was an Intelligence Analyst for seven years. Well, I still am, technically," said Ella.

Byford shut down his screen and looked her way for the first time since arriving in Delaware. It seemed she had his attention now.

"You still are? You're not a field agent?"

"Not really. I was a guinea pig for the new recruitment system. They pulled me from Intelligence about six months ago and partnered me with Agent Ripley. Whenever there's no active case, I go back to my old job, but I haven't done a whole lot there this year, actually."

Byford squinted like he was focusing on a tiny molecule on Ella's forehead. "That's odd. I thought they were partnering me with a true field agent."

The words stung a little. Ella acknowledged the pain and dealt with it. She let it go. She didn't want to get off to a bad start with this guy.

"I've got four cases solved. All the ones I've worked on, actually. Let's hope we can get another in the books."

"I see," Byford said. "I'm sure Agent Ripley played a considerable role, no?"

Frustration rose up. Was this guy trying to undermine her? She kept a level head, still. "She certainly did. We both did."

"Why did your relationship cease?" Byford asked. "Seems strange to part a successful duo."

Ella toyed with the notion of lying, something that was fast becoming commonplace in her life. No, there'd already been enough of that. She went for broke.

"We fell out. I did something and she didn't approve. Then it went downhill."

"Oh," Byford looked a little taken aback. "I'm sorry to hear that. I won't inquire further."

Ella thanked her lucky stars she didn't have to tell him the finer details. At least she'd addressed the issue without lying, she thought. "And what about you?"

"I started in ballistics, then moved to terrorism for ten years. Two years ago, I moved into less specialized field work. I worked a few murder cases, some of which are still ongoing. Now I'm making my first visit to Delaware."

Quite a resume, Ella thought, but she wanted to know about the man, not the career. "How come you left terrorism and came here? Did you want to track down serial killers? Are you interested in them?"

"Not at all, but they come with the territory. How come you were chosen to do this job?" Byford asked. "Not to make assumptions, but you don't look the field type."

Ella was getting a little concerned now. Did this guy have something against her? "Ripley picked me because I have a photographic memory."

Byford stared out the window then turned back to Ella. "A photographic memory? How does that help?"

Ella pursed her lips together to stop her from saying something she shouldn't. "Because serial killers follow patterns. I've committed every piece of serial killer information to memory. Names, dates, victim info, methodologies, death sites. It's all up here," she tapped her head. "Not on purpose, I should admit. It happened by accident, but it got me here."

"Very interesting. I'm impressed," Byford said. His words didn't match the look on his face. Maybe he just wasn't very expressive. "What do you think of this case?" he asked.

Newark, Delaware, looked like a cozy city from where she sat. She spotted some nice European architecture and lots of family stores. It didn't have that big city vibe and that was a bonus.

"I think we're dealing with an organized psychopath," Ella said. "I think our unsub knows exactly what he's doing. He doesn't make

25

mistakes. He has a goal, and nothing will stop him achieving it. What about you?"

"These coins. I don't know what to make of them. Are they symbolic of money problems? Maybe these men were in debt to our killer? Or is it something more sinister, something that doesn't make sense to regular people?"

"We'll figure it out. The one advantage we have is that this man is organized, which means his thoughts are organized too. He isn't schizophrenic or psychotic. The coins have a verifiable, understandable meaning and we'll search hell and high water to uncover it."

"Have coins appeared in any other serial cases?" Byford asked.

"Not in the same way as this. The closest one that comes to mind is Daniel LaPlante, a stalker who left a trail of coins in a girl's" house to let her know he'd been there. Eyes are a different story. There are two major serial killers who focused on their victims' eyes. Charles Albright and Andrei Chikatilo. But again, not like this."

"So, we're covering new ground," Byford said.

"Looks like it." Ella's phone buzzed. She checked it and found a message from Mark.

Did you get there safely? X

Ella replied. *Yep, the eagle has landed. They've teamed me with a guy named Byford. Do you know him? x*

On their chat screen, Ella saw Mark was typing already. The message came through.

Who? Never heard of him. What's his deal?

Ella's turn. *He's nice enough, but he seems a bit closed off. We'll see. How are you doing? X*

She expected another quick reply, but nothing came. She waited on the screen for Mark to come online. It took about a minute for him to respond.

So you're spending the next week with a guy? Great. Well, have fun.

Had she said something wrong? What was Mark's problem? She couldn't help who she was partnered with, and she wasn't in any position to refuse the director or make her own demands. Mark would come around once he realized there was no danger of anything happening. It wasn't like Byford was a chiseled young stud, and even if he was, didn't Mark trust her?

She hoped this jealousy thing was a one-off, but really, she shouldn't have to hope.

***

They arrived at their destination at just after midday. A pleasant street hidden away from public view, sitting between a small, wooded area at the front and a cemetery backing onto the rear. It was isolated, but not isolated enough to suggest the victim was chosen for their solitude.

Yellow crime scene tape barred the pathway up to the house. One officer stood by and dissected the new arrivals with a cold stare. Byford led the way.

"Agent Byford and Agent Dark with the FBI," he said to the officer. "We've been called in to assist." They held up their badges for inspection. The officer waved them through without a word.

At the top of the path, another officer came out of the house wearing a mask and gloves. "Feds?" he asked. "That you guys?"

"That's us, sir," Byford said. "And you are?"

"Sheriff Hunter with the NDPD. I'm the one who called in for help." He took off his protective equipment.

He was a middle-aged man, around fifty Ella thought. He had gray hair and a strong physique that contrasted the wrinkles on his forehead. "Can you talk us through what happened?" she asked.

Sheriff Hunter breathed in the spring air. It was probably a great relief after consuming the scent of death.

"Yeah, we got the call around three this morning. The victim's wife, a lovely woman named Tessa Loveridge, had come home from a night shift and found her husband, Jimmy, dead in his chair. She didn't see him at first. Thought he was just sleeping. Then she tried to wake him up and saw... everything."

Ella's stomach tied up when she played the scene out in her head. She'd also found a loved one dead in their bed. She knew that the victim's wife would spend the rest of her life replaying the scene every time she felt vulnerable. It was a natural defense mechanism: pulling out the worst nightmare you could to numb the others.

"Where's the victim's wife right now?" Ella asked. She wanted to meet her but understood if she didn't want to be around. She'd probably never be able to come back here again.

"Staying with a relative for now. Best to leave her be for a while. She was still in hysterics when she left."

"Is the crime scene untouched?" Byford asked.

"No. The croakers already took the body, but everything else is as is." The sheriff put a roach filter in his mouth as he rolled a cigarette.

"The who?" Byford asked.

"Coroners," Ella said.

Sheriff Hunter sparked up. "Sorry. Cop slang. You'll get used to it around here. Grab a mask and gloves off the side and take a look."

They did. Ella entered into a kitchen and put herself in the wife's shoes. She'd be home from work, tired, probably looking forward to kicking her feet up. She walked through the long kitchen then round into the living area. A sofa lay against one wall with a single chair on the other side. It was obvious where the murder had taken place.

"Holy smokes, that's a lot of blood," Byford said. "That means the laceration was made while the victim was alive."

Ella thought about how it might be possible to pull off such a task. "So, our killer snuck up behind Jimmy and slit his throat, all without him moving."

Byford rubbed his chin. "Maybe Jimmy was sleeping? We don't know what time he was killed. It could have been right before his wife came home in the early hours."

"Could very well have been," Ella said. She imagined the victim in place, sitting there peacefully, unaware there was an intruder within grabbing distance. "How did he get in? That's the next question." Ella walked around the house, finding a conservatory just off the living room. Byford joined her.

"Looks like that garden backs on the cemetery at the back. He could easily get in through there."

"Agreed. That's the route I'd take. He could stay invisible until he got to the door." Ella checked the conservatory door leading out into the garden. Open.

"Looks like we have our answer," Byford said. "Tragic, really."

"It's a damn shame, but he might have broken this door open. Let's not assume Jimmy and Tessa just left it open."

"We need to talk to Tessa, get her statement."

Footsteps sounded behind them and Sheriff Hunter appeared. Ella smelled the lingering scent of stale smoke. "He must have come over the back. This door was open when we got here. When'll people learn to lock their doors, huh?"

Ella refrained from agreeing. Blaming the victim for their carelessness was a cop out. The sheriff held up a small plastic bag in front of the agents.

"You might want to take a look at these," he continued. Ella took them and held them to the light.

"The coins from the eyes."

"Yeah. I'm not seeing anything special about them myself. I thought a better mind than me might catch something though."

Two silver half-dollars, both identical. The face of the coin featured the side portrait of a very familiar image.

"Is that Kennedy?" Byford asked.

"That's Kennedy alright," said the sheriff.

LIBERTY. IN GOD WE TRUST. 1964.

"1964? This coin must be a collectible," said Ella.

"It is a collectible but not exactly rare. You can probably pick this up off the Internet for five dollars these days."

"You already checked?" Ella asked.

"I had a quick look, but I had a few special coins myself back in the day. Kennedy '64s were common as mud."

The coins were rusted with age. Only a glimmer of silver was left on them. "Can we get them reviewed? Appraised? There might be something on them that tells us where they're from."

"Once they've gone for fingerprinting, I'll see what I can do," Hunter said.

Ella pictured the killer placing the coins on Jimmy's eyes, lodging them in with force. The brief flicker of light from them would have given the impression of life, like sparkling eyes forced to watch their own deaths. Maybe that was it, Ella thought. A dead body propped up to look alive, only for the finder to suddenly realize the grim truth. Without hope, there was no true despair.

"What do you think the coins mean?" Sheriff Hunter asked.

Ella handed them back to him. "Right now, I don't know, but I'm going to find out."

CHAPTER FIVE

Their new office for the foreseeable future was a single room at the NDPD precinct in downtown Newark. Ella knew the process pretty well by now. Sheriff Hunter led them through the open floor plan, past an endless clutter of desks into their rooms at the back. Ella and Byford got a few discerning looks as they came through, but most of the officers offered smiles and, well-wishes as they passed by. In most cases, local officers were happy for the FBI to join their investigation because it meant less work on the whole.

Ella set up her rig in the gray office. The rectangular window offered a glimpse of the Delaware streets below. Distracting, but it was better than looking at blank walls. Byford set up opposite her.

The casefile was around thirty pages thick. Ella began reading everything about the first victim.

"Alan Yates, 59 years old. He lived eight miles from the second victim," Ella said aloud. "Everything looks the same here. Same killing method, same modus operandi, same signature. The victims were even pretty close in age too."

Byford tapped his pen between his teeth. "You know, after seeing that house, it doesn't look like Jimmy was struggling for money. They seemed pretty well-off."

"Yeah, same with the first victim judging by these photos too. Their house looks pretty modest. So we can rule out the possibility of debt?"

"Well, I wouldn't want to make any assumptions, but it looks like it."

"I agree," Ella said. "This is too theatric to be about debt. If he wanted payback on these people, he wouldn't stage them so specifically. He would just off them and be done. His message isn't meant for the victims; it's meant for the rest of the world."

"How do you mean?" Byford asked, squinting his eyes.

Ella remembered what Edis told her about Byford's past. He wasn't so good at getting in the heads of these people.

"What I mean is this unsub isn't killing for the usual reason killers do, which is sexual gratification. If he was, there would have been more mutilation, so we can rule out the possibility of him being a sadist. These murders are warnings. They're his way of showing off. He's saying *look what I can do, and you can't stop me.*"

"I see. So he's almost a domestic terrorist. Inciting fear for his own power trip."

Ella hadn't thought about it that way. "I suppose. Good observation. This should be right up your street then."

"What did these men do for work? Maybe there's a connection there."

Ella leafed through the file. "Victim one was retired. Victim two was an antiques dealer." Not much to go on. A dead end.

Sheriff Hunter opened their office door and peered his head in. "You guys set up okay?"

"Fine, thank you," Byford said. "What's the coffee situation around here?"

Ella laughed. She had wanted to ask the same question but didn't want to be rude.

"There's a machine down the corridor but it costs a few nickels. And speaking of nickels," Hunter placed a small plastic bag on their table. "I thought you might want to see these. Just got them back from the lab."

Inside the bag were two rusted old bronze coins. The faces had all but perished. "We got them cleaned up because we couldn't make out any of the markings."

"The coins from the first victim," Ella said. She could make out the number one, a small inscription of a leaf and an indecipherable symbol. Then it hit her. "Oh, wow. Is that kanji? Japanese coins?"

"Nail on the head," Hunter said. "One thousand yen, apparently. Now this one *is* worth a decent amount in the collector scene."

Byford picked up the bag and studied it. He held it right up close to his nose. "Am I seeing this right?" he asked. "Or are my eyes playing tricks on me in my old age?"

"What do you mean?" Hunter asked.

Byford ran his finger over an inscription along the edge of the coin. "The year. It's the same as the other coins."

Hunter took it. "Well, bone me sideways. You're right."

"It's from 1964?" Ella asked.

"Yup. I guess we couldn't see it because it was rusted to all hell."

A connection. A year. But what did it mean? Ella's first thought was how they could use it to draw this unsub out.

"What do you think it means?" the sheriff asked.

31

"What if it's from the same collection? Someone who collects coins from this year?" Byford said.

The sheriff scratched his stubble. "Gotta be careful. 1964 was a big year for coins. Must have been a million new coins that year because it was an Olympic year."

Still, it was something, Ella thought. "Are both bodies at the coroner's now?" she asked.

"Yeah, you want to go down?"

"Please," Ella said. "There's something I need to see."

***

Years ago, Ella would have been nervous at the sight of seeing decomposed bodies close up, but now, she'd seen enough corpses to last a lifetime.

The Newark Coroner's Office was located inside the city hospital. The two agents entered the hospital via a rear fire door which led almost directly to the restricted autopsy room. Down a spiraling staircase, they waited outside the steel entranceway until access was granted.

"What is it you want to see?" Byford asked.

"A few things. A killer like this would want to spend considerable time with his victims, ideally while they were alive. He'd want to relish it for as long as possible. I find it hard to believe he'd be in and out within a few minutes."

Byford turned to her, prompting her to continue. She realized she hadn't answered his question.

"I want to see if there's something we've missed. Like maybe a sign of a struggle, or additional wounds we might have missed. It all helps paint a picture of his personality and his motivations."

A deafening buzz announced their acceptance into the autopsy room. Ella pushed her way in, adjusting her eyes to the heavy fluorescent lights overhead.

The masked technician peered up from his medical table, dressed head to toe in dirty white regalia. In front of him, the same dismembered bodies Ella had seen in the photos earlier lay on two steel gurneys. No longer did they portray human figures, and instead were filed next to each other in a neat line, together in death. She thought of their poor loved ones and how they'd remember these men forever like this.

"Welcome folks," the coroner announced, "I'm Doctor Sharp. You might want to put some surgical masks on before you head over here. They don't smell too pretty."

Ella and Byford obliged, pulling two masks and two pairs of gloves from a box on the table beside them. "Can you talk us through what you've found?" Ella asked, hoping there'd be some recent developments.

Doctor Sharp picked up a surgical pointer and put on a pair of glasses. He was only a young man, Ella thought, barely out of his twenties. It was rare to see someone so youthful in this profession. A young man in an old man's game. How the world progressed.

"Alan Yates, 59 years old," Doctor Sharp said. He pointed the tool at the incision on the victim's neck. "This incision was the cause of death, as you can probably guess. I found traces of mild steel along the wound, meaning it was made with a standard carbon knife. Nothing specific."

Ella cursed. That was one avenue they couldn't explore.

Doctor Sharp moved over to Jimmy Loveridge. He pointed to the same location. "This incision is almost identical. Same depth, same force applied, same weapon. It's rare to find two wounds so similar. Usually, uncontrollable factors determine the differences, but this guy knew what he was doing."

"Were the victims conscious when they were killed?" Byford asked.

"It's difficult to say. Because it would have taken them a few seconds to pass out, they would have woken up if they were sleeping. But to get precise cuts like these, I'd say he was able to spend a few seconds finding the right spot. If I was a betting man, I'd say they were sleeping when he found them."

Ella inspected the bodies from top to bottom. Alan Yates's skin had faded to a sickly yellow color and blemishes were beginning to form. His dead eyes stared up at the green-tinted ceiling above. Ella checked the wrists and feet, finding nothing but putrefied skin. That gnawing dread surged back into her veins, the same one that appeared whenever she was presented with specimens of premature ends. The fragility of life, she thought. She welcomed the sensation, because even in these grim surroundings, it made her feel human. She never wanted to reach the point where she couldn't feel something from seeing human remains, and she wasn't, at least not yet.

"Were there any ligature marks?" Ella asked.

"None at all. The only marks were these neck wounds. I'm sorry."

33

"Did you check inside the body?" Ella asked. "I know it's an odd question."

Doctor Sharp laughed. "It's fine, and yes, I did. I scanned the internal for any foreign bodies and there was nothing inside. No coins, if that's what you're thinking."

Ella felt sudden nausea. Something told her there was more to these bodies than the crime scene photos showed, but it turns out that wasn't the case. The disappointment came hard. Maybe she didn't know this killer as well as she thought she did.

"What about the eyes?" Byford asked. "Anything to note there?"

Doctor Sharp shook his head. "I heard about the coins, but they'd been removed before the bodies got here. I found light tracings of nickel and silver around the eyes, so your killer most likely brute forced them in there."

Ella felt she'd reached a dead end. There was nothing here to go on. She thought about where to go next but couldn't think of a new avenue to explore. She made some notes in her pad. "Thank you doctor. You've been a great help."

Doctor Sharp covered both bodies with sheets. "I knew him, you know?"

She looked up from her notes. "Did you?"

"Yeah. Alan Yates. He was a popular man around here."

She felt something. Like this could break new ground. "Was he? How come?"

"Quite a philanthropist. The guy had some serious money. He donated a portion to the hospital if I remember rightly."

"Oh, I didn't know. This must be doubly hard for you then."

"It's a tough one, I won't lie. It's quite ironic as well. The coins."

Ella and Byford exchanged a glance. "How do you mean?" Ella asked.

Doctor Sharp had a sudden look of hesitation, like he shouldn't have opened his mouth. "Sorry, I didn't mean it like that. Not ironic. Just… weird."

"What's strange about it? Because he had money?" asked Byford.

"No. Well, sort of. I mean because of his old job."

"Job?" asked Ella. She suddenly realized the casefile didn't mention what Alan Yates did before he retired.

"Yeah, he retired real early because he didn't need to work, but before that he was a big-time banker."

There was the connection, the link she desperately needed. "Oh my God, really? His notes didn't mention that." She caught Byford's eye.

"A banker and an antiques dealer, left with old coins in their eyes. That can't be a coincidence."

The first real adrenaline rush kicked in. This was why she loved being out here. She was breaking down the walls and getting into this killer's head. Byford didn't seem as excited as her.

"You've been a great help, doctor. If you think of anything else, please let us know."

On the way out, Ella explained her thoughts to her new partner.

"You see the link?" she asked. "That's huge."

Byford shrugged. "I don't know. It's tenuous, not to mention it means our last theory was wrong."

They needed to speak to someone close to the victims, Ella thought. Alan didn't have any close family in the area so that only left one person on their radar: Jimmy Loveridge's wife. If they could dig into Jimmy's life and find someone linked to both Jimmy and Alan, they had a shot of finding their unsub.

"Yeah, it does, but that's what happens. These weren't random attacks. They were targeted. I think our killer is sacrificing these men. Come on, we need to talk to Jimmy's wife."

CHAPTER SIX

If these victims were targeted, Ella needed to know more about them. Byford did the driving with Ella in the passenger seat. They went straight from the Medical Examiner's office to Pike Creek about twelve miles away.

The address was a single-story home just off Cherry Street, a plaque on the wall identifying it as Orchard House. Next to it, it said *entrance to 109 round the back*. This was the home of Tessa's sister, where she was staying for the time being.

The agents followed the stone pathway round to the back and opened the gate. Ella searched for a buzzer but didn't find one. She knocked and waited. From behind the frosted glass, a blurry figure emerged.

"Who is it?" the blur asked.

"Good day, we're with the FBI. Could we please speak with Tessa Loveridge?"

Ella saw the figure's reluctance through the fuzzy barrier. The door unbolted and they came face to face with a middle-aged woman, gray hair around a plain face.

"Hi, are you Tessa?" Byford asked.

"No. I'm her sister. Should you really be around here so soon?"

"We need to talk to her. It's a matter of urgency," Byford said. The comment caught Ella by surprise. Very abrupt, she thought.

"We're sorry we have to be here," Ella jumped in, "but our best chances of catching whoever did this lie with Tessa. We mean no disrespect being here so soon."

The woman sighed and moved out of the way. She called the agents through into her home. They entered into a carpeted hallway with a lounge to their right.

"Tessa, you've got visitors," the woman said. She pointed towards the front room and the agents followed her cue. Ella walked in to find a woman curled up on a brown sofa. Stale tears clung to her cheeks and washed her makeup down her face. A cup of coffee sat on the table beside her, but it was stone cold judging by the look of it.

"Tessa, I'm Agent Dark and this is Agent Byford. We're with the FBI. Would you be willing to talk to us for five minutes? We promise we won't keep you long."

Tessa had shoulder-length brown hair and a figure that had seen plenty of gym time. She looked in peak physical condition, but emotional was a different story. She nodded her head without even looking at the agents.

"Okay," she said.

Ella and Byford lowered themselves onto a two-seater couch on the other side of the room. Tessa slowly sat up, turned off the TV and tied back her hair. "Sorry. I look like shit."

"Please don't apologize. You look fine."

"Yeah, right." Tessa sniveled and wiped her nose. The undersides of her eyes were red raw. "What do you want to know?"

"Could you talk us through what happened last night?" asked Ella

Tessa took a moment to compose herself. She kept her gaze on the floor as she spoke. "I got home from work about two-thirty in the morning. Night shift. I'm a nurse at the hospital. When I walked in, I walked past Jim in his chair. The lights were off, so I guessed he'd fallen asleep in front of the TV."

"Alright. Then what?" Byford asked. Ella was getting a little annoyed with his hasty tone.

"I went upstairs to get changed and I found an insect in the bathroom. I went to get Jim to kill it, and that's when I realized he was... gone." Tessa wiped her eyes as new tears came.

"I can't imagine what that must have been like. We're so sorry," said Ella, showing sympathy before Byford blurted out something abrupt.

"It was hell. I can't believe it. I think I went into shock. I called the police and ran out into the street."

Ella knew that Tessa's first thought at the time was that the killer might still be in the house. A lot of people didn't want to admit it, but it was human nature to worry that you were next in line. "What can you tell us about your husband? He seems like a good man."

"The best," Tessa nodded. "When I got home, he hadn't put the trash out and I remember getting mad at him. God, I feel like such a fool. Now, I'll never get to be mad at him ever again." Tessa's words were punctuated with sobs. She cupped her hands around her face. Ella jumped out of her seat and sat next to her. It was an expected reaction on her part and Tessa needed to know it was okay to let it all out.

"Jimmy seemed like a great guy, and you had many happy years together. Trust me, when you're better you'll remember nothing but the good times. I've been there myself." Ella rubbed Tessa's arm.

"Have you?" Tessa asked into her hand-mask.

"Yes. When I was a little girl, I found my dad dead in his bed. I won't lie, it was the worst night of my life, but now I'm just thankful I got to spend a few years with him before he passed. Pretty soon, you'll think the same."

Tessa came around. She wiped away the residue on her face with her dressing gown sleeve. "That's horrible. But you know how I feel."

Ella looked over at Byford. He looked incredibly uncomfortable. She guessed empathy wasn't his strong suit.

"It's gonna be hard for a while but you've got people around you. You'll still struggle with it, probably for the rest of your life, but it gets easier. And if someone tells you to *be strong,* tell them to get lost because you can cry all you want, whenever you want, okay?" Ella thought Tessa smiled but it was hard to tell.

"Thanks. Nice to know I'm not alone."

Ella stayed put. "You're not. And if you tell us everything we need to know, we'll catch the son of a bitch who did this to Jimmy. We promise."

Tessa reached out and drank from her cold coffee. It seemed to perk her up. "Not much to tell. He's a simple man. He's been an antiques dealer since he was a teenager. If it's old and rusty, he'll sell it," she smiled.

"A true carny," Ella said, praying Tessa wouldn't take offense.

"Oh yes. Carny to the bone."

"How was his business doing?" Byford asked from across the room. Tessa caught his eye.

"It was fine. The thing about antiques is that you only need to sell a few to make good money. Some of that junk went for thousands of dollars."

"Did Jimmy have any enemies in his trade? Maybe competitors?"

Tessa thought about it for a second. The head shaking began. "Not really. Antique dealers are few and far between. He had some trouble with a few pawn shops, and had he had a few crazy customers, but nobody that would kill him. Jim was a respected man."

"What was his trouble with the pawn shops?" Ella asked.

"It was only really one pawn shop. Aces & Eights on the high street. Sometimes Jimmy and the owner would have fallings out, but it was minor stuff. They were friends, really."

It didn't seem likely, but it was worth keeping it in mind, Ella thought. Plus, there was the money link. Ella got out her phone and pulled up a few pictures.

"Please don't think of this as insensitive, but did your husband ever trade these kinds of coins?" Ella showed Tessa the coins pulled from Alan and Jimmy's eyes.

Tessa glanced at them and then straight back to the floor. "No. Coins aren't his thing. He does furniture, ornaments, clocks, some weird religious stuff. One of his old jokes was *'there's no money in coins.'*"

Ella wasn't sure she heard Tessa correctly. Suddenly, her thoughts went down a dark path, and for a moment she was transported to a different world. Here, these murders took on a much more sinister hue.

"Does the name Alan Yates mean anything to you?" Byford chipped in before Ella could speak first.

Tessa wiped her nose. "No, sorry. Who is that?"

"Another victim of this unsub," said Byford.

"Un-what? What's that?"

"Unsub. It means unknown subject."

"You mean Jim wasn't the only one?"

Ella was surprised Tessa hadn't already heard about it. "No. Another gentleman was murdered three days before your husband was," she said. "This is a serial case."

The announcement induced new fear in Tessa. She suddenly pressed herself into the arm of the sofa. "A serial killer? In this town? What if he comes after me next?"

If Mia was here, she'd throw her a stern look about now. She always told her off for revealing details she shouldn't. "He won't come after you. You're safe here."

"How do you know that?" Tessa said. "You don't know who this guy is. He could be anyone. What am I gonna do, live here forever?"

"Serial killers don't work like that. Your husband was chosen at random. This isn't about anyone in particular." Ella wasn't sure if she was telling the truth or not, but right now Tessa needed comfort more than anything.

"Well, stupid me. Forgive me for not knowing that."

"Sorry, I'm just trying to say you'll be fine."

"Fine?" Tessa shouted. "Are you out of your mind? My husband was murdered *in my house,* and you think I'm gonna be fine?"

Ella felt this escalating. Tessa was getting hysterical. Understandable, but it would just make her feel worse in the long run. Ella didn't want that. Tessa jumped out of her chair.

39

"I've been a widow for a day, and you come in here asking me questions, why don't you…"

Byford leaped from his seat and came in between Ella and Tessa. He took Tessa's hand.

"Mrs. Loveridge, my partner meant no harm. You understand it's difficult for us to navigate these conversations sometimes." Tessa pushed Byford's arm away. He held up his palms to her. "Please, we're here to do a job. A thankless one at that."

Tessa backed up to the far wall. She dropped down into a sitting position and the tears came again.

"I'm sorry," she sobbed. "I've lost the only man I've ever been with. I don't know what to do."

Poor woman, Ella thought. As hard as it was for the investigators, it was a million times more difficult for the victims" families.

"Don't do anything," Byford said. "Just keep going. Sit in silence for hours. Cry all you have to. Go through old photos. Just because he's not here in the flesh, doesn't mean he isn't alive in your memories."

Ella could barely believe these words were coming from Byford. She'd only known him a day but she didn't think he was capable of such emotion.

"You're right. Forgive me. I didn't mean to lash out," Tessa said. She crawled to her feet then sat beside Ella. "Thank you for the words of encouragement. Both of you."

Byford reached out and shook her hand. "If you think of anything else that might assist us, please contact us at the NDPD."

"I will. Please find whoever did this."

"We're doing everything we can, ma'am, and your information will certainly help us."

Ella followed Byford out the door, saying her goodbyes to Tessa and her sister on the way out. They headed to the car in silence.

"Tricky one," Byford said.

Ella started up the engine. Interviews like this always felt surreal. "Thank you for stepping in there," she said.

"That's what partners are for. Do we have any family to interview on victim one's side?"

They rolled off the driveway and back onto the road. "No. Alan Yates lived on his own. A neighbor found him."

"So I guess it's back to research."

"Yeah, but I have something I want to look at. Let's head to the precinct."

CHAPTER SEVEN

The feelings coursed through Ella, sensations that grew exponentially. She paced around her office like a caged animal. Byford ignored her as he typed away on his laptop. About now, Mia would have pushed her to spill her theories. What she needed right now was another mind to bounce ideas off, shape and mold them into actionable plans. She craved an expert's ear to filter her muddled thoughts, but Byford didn't seem at all interested.

But still, she couldn't be too frustrated with him. He'd saved her from a hysterical woman a few hours ago.

She began writing on the whiteboard, but her thoughts strayed too far to make any coherent notes.

"Ella, what's wrong?" Byford asked, finally. At last, she had an invitation to bounce her ideas off him.

"Did you hear what Tessa said her husband sold at his shop? Weird religious things."

"Yes, and?"

"I checked the store online and found what she was talking about. Look at this." She turned her laptop around to show a row of miniature statues. One was a hand missing two fingers, another was some kind of demonic ghoul, another was a deformed fetus.

"Not something I'd associate with antiques, but I'm sure someone would purchase them," Byford said.

"These aren't religious things; they're occult relics," said Ella. "What if we're looking at this all wrong?"

"Wrong how?"

"I've been thinking about how rare it is for a serial killer to knowingly leave something behind at the scene. Other than items of convenience like murder weapons, it's pretty much unheard of. Leaving something behind just gives police more evidence to work with, so these coins must be the most important part of his ritual."

Byford sat back in his chair. "Right, but what's this got to do with religious relics?"

41

"Because of the serial killers who left behind physical items, a lot of them were motivated by religion, Satanism, occult beliefs. There was a guy named Luke Woodham, a so-called Satanist who left behind goat horns. There was Michael Hardman who left behind ripped Bibles. Michael Kelly who left behind masks. I could go on."

Byford seemed impressed. "So you think this has to do with what, Satanism?"

"No, not quite that. But coins have a long history with occult beliefs. I've been reading about it since we got back. Have you heard of Charon's Obol? It's an ancient Greek practice where people used to put coins over dead people's eyes to take them to the underworld. Ancient Egyptians used to put coins over the eyes of the dead to shield them from the horrors of the afterlife. It's all there."

"So, why's this guy doing it?"

Ella got frustrated again. "I don't know, but it's too much of a coincidence to ignore. There's also a load of occult religions that do similar things. A church called The Final Judgment mummified their dead with coins in their hands so they could pay something called the boatman's toll in the afterlife."

"Ella, I don't know. It sounds very farfetched. Could it not just be that this unsub is a psychopath with a twisted world view? Or perhaps he's just insane? This all sounds very specific."

Ella dropped down in her seat, the theories burning her brain. There were too many to just focus on one and that was the problem. She didn't know where to begin, and she couldn't consume everything she needed to know about these bizarre practices on her own. Even worse, Byford didn't seem like he wanted to entertain this idea at all.

Mia would have.

"So, what do *you* suggest we do? Because I'm not seeing many leads here."

"Neither am I," Byford said, "and your outlandish claims aren't producing any leads either. This is all just conjecture. Even if he *is* doing something along these lines, how does it help us find him?"

Ella couldn't believe what she was hearing. "How does it help us find him? There are a hundred ways this could help us find him. We could search for other practitioners of these religions in the area. We could try and find an online presence of his on a community forum. We could track down more potential victims."

Byford stood up with enough force to push his chair back. "You do that then, but I think it's a waste of time."

"A waste of time?" Ella said. "To help save lives?"

"I'm all for saving lives, but I'm not one for speculation. We have to go off the *evidence*."

"And what evidence do we have? Both victims had a tenuous connection to coins. Antiques and money. That's it. Pretty much anyone who works in these fields could be a potential target. That's too many people. We need to narrow it down."

Ella didn't like this. It felt like they were at two opposing ends of the track. When she argued with Mia, it was always for the good of the case. Byford seemed to have a reluctance to dig any further than the surface.

"You could always suggest something," Ella said, her voice a little rougher than she anticipated.

"I am," Byford said as he moved towards the door. "I'm going to get a drink and clear my head because you've filled it with nonsense. Then I'm going to come back and do actual detective work rather than making outrageous guesses."

He left the room, slamming the door in the process.

Ella stared at the gray door, dumbstruck. Had her partner really just walked out on her? All because she was trying to make headway in a murder investigation?

She pushed back her hair and then rubbed the disbelief from her face. The last thing she needed right now was more conflict. She buried her head in her notes again, but the words on the page just skated past her pupils, not going beyond the eyes to the brain. She couldn't focus. Her palms began to sweat, and she suddenly craved another soul to confide in, even if it was just to talk about something mundane. Anything. She just wanted to know someone out there was on her side.

Mark was the first name that jumped into her head, but she didn't want to deal with his paranoia right now.

Was there anyone else?

One person, she thought. One person who could help her. The only partner who always knew exactly what to say to make things right.

Ella pulled out her phone and found her recent call lists. The phone would probably ring out again, but she had to try. She dialed Mia's mobile again.

Please answer, she thought. *For God's sake, I need you.*

***

Mia Ripley sat alone in a Manhattan bar after leaving Melissa back at the local precinct. She needed to get away from her and clear her head. She'd been off the booze for three weeks now so she drank what she referred to as a virgin whiskey and coke. It wasn't quite the good stuff but it was better than nothing.

Her phone chimed on the table in front of her, and for what seemed like the millionth time this week, Ella's name flashed up on the screen.

"Rookie, you gotta leave me alone," she said aloud. "We're done."

But what would happen if she answered? Would Ella apologize her heart out like she usually did? Would she try and justify what she did? Or was she looking for something else?

Mia couldn't deny the rookie's capabilities. She made a fantastic partner, even if she was a little reckless. But all of her partners had their flaws. Hadn't her first one been high off his rocker every time they were together? Hadn't that weird woman she was partnered with in '06 tried to sleep with her son? Yes, they were all imperfect, but none of them kept real secrets from her. None of them conversed with the man who triggered nightmares and crippling self-doubt. The man who took everything from her and made her question her own abilities.

It was an unforgivable act. There was no going back from here.

Mia had already heard about the serial case down in Delaware, and she knew Ella had been assigned to it with her new guy. An odd duo, she thought, and no doubt Byford would be getting on her nerves by now. Mia had her own thoughts about the case, although they were admittedly based on the bare facts and nothing more. The coins were a crucial part of the killer's identity and the men were surrogates for something much bigger. By now, the rookie should have figured that out.

Or had she? Had Mia's teachings left their mark or was the rookie clueless without her by her side? When they first got together, Ella wasn't very skilled at getting inside these killers' heads, but on the last case she was analyzing them like a veteran profiler.

No, the rookie would be fine. She had to be. Mia was never going to be by her side forever, so it was time she learned to handle these things on her own.

Her name flashed up again. It would be twelve long seconds before it stopped. Mia hovered her index finger over the green *ANSWER* button and toyed with the idea of talking to her one more time, maybe just to swap ideas on her case. Hell, maybe the rookie would have some insights to share on her Manhattan case too.

But then she remembered the letter from Tobias, the tidal wave of spilled secrets drowning her out. Mia would never forget that feeling. It was like reliving the past all over again, that night when Tobias made

44

her burn all of the evidence she'd found. She'd faced countless criminals since then, been at their mercy more times than she could count, but that night with Tobias Campbell was the only time she felt true despair.

She might be a product of the past, but she wasn't going to be a prisoner of it. It was time to move on. Her short stint with Ella had been a memorable one for a host of reasons, but she was more than willing to let sleeping dogs lie. Time to move on. New partners, new adventures.

But she'd be lying to herself if she didn't miss the rookie's occasional wild theories.

CHAPTER EIGHT

He unlocked the door to the forgotten room in his house and was suddenly reminded of an old story. On his deathbed, Johann Sebastian Bach asked an organist to play one of his symphonies. The organist stopped before he finished the piece, so Bach leaped from his bed, rushed to his piano and finished it. Bach couldn't live with an unfinished melody, and neither could he. That's why he had to do what he was doing.

His forgotten room had gone untouched for the longest time. Dust and cobwebs lined the walls like peeling wallpaper, and there was a distinct smell that reminded him of the old man himself. It felt like there was still a part of him here, watching from between the boards, ready to appear like a phantom and reprimand him for his wrongdoings.

He'd never added up exactly how much money this collection was worth. Maybe a few thousand dollars, nothing really worth pursuing considering the amount of time that had gone into acquiring the collection. The coins sat in bags and jars, some in frames and some stacked high. There were too many to count, some from the Victorian era, some from faraway lands. But the best and most treasured ones were in the glass case.

No doubt the collection would bring great pleasure to an enthusiast of the hobby, but what he was doing was worth much more. You could put a price on gold-plated war memorial coin from 1950, but there was no price for vengeance. No price for taking back years of lost youth and innocence. Two down and plenty more to come.

Who would be next? There was no shortage of potential targets. It could be the old man from the bank who always made him feel stupid when he made deposits. It could be that bitch coin collector who was always tracking down those rare British pennies.

He circled the room, taking in the sights and auras. This room had been sealed for God knows how long. He'd even put filler in the door cracks so he couldn't get in here if he tried.

But the past few months, something changed. The room called to him like a siren's song, luring him back to the forbidden relics within.

He wondered if he'd feel different when he saw the coins, or would he still harbor the same rage and fury he felt as a youngster?

Armed with a sledge hammer, he'd smashed down the door and walked in like a Viking ready to pillage. He'd forgotten just how many coins there were in here. In his head, there were only a hundred or so, but now he realized there were thousands upon thousands. It only then dawned on him just how long it had taken to acquire such a vast collection. A lost lifetime's worth. Now, it was time to make up for it.

He picked up a 1942 Nazi coin off the table and rolled it around in his fingers. No, this one wouldn't do. Too specific. He found a stack of Nigerian coins from 1970, all but eroded to dust. No, he needed something that sent a real message.

He lifted up the glass table and chose one of the so-called favorites. A Chinese coin from the Shen-Si Province, still with visible flecks of gold. He checked the year.

1964.

Perfect.

Now, who was going to be the lucky recipient?

CHAPTER NINE

Ella had been alone for ten minutes now. God knows where Byford had gone. She wanted to apologize and get back on track because being on two different wavelengths wasn't going to get them anywhere.

Mia hadn't answered her phone the two times she'd tried. Maybe it was never going to happen. Mia had erased her from her life and there was nothing she could do other than show up on her doorstep. And even then, who's to say she wouldn't just get the door slammed in her face? That was the most likely option.

She tried to forget about the Mia situation and focus on the case. Even if Byford wasn't going to buy her theory, she was going to pursue it regardless. This killer had a religious fixation, be it occultism, Christianity, Satanism or anything else that fell under the banner of blind devotion. It had to be the case. That's what the pattern showed.

Ella's phone pinged on the table. Mark had finally decided to reply. *How are things going?*

She typed her response. *Up and down. I'm trying to figure this guy out, but he keeps throwing me curveballs. Working on a new theory. Are you doing okay? x*

Her laptop showed a screen dedicated to the forgotten religion of Santeria. According to her research, Santerians believed that certain coins contained ashes of the gods and placing them among the dead would make them targets of the creatures of hell. And in addition to this cruel practice, Santerians also carried out ritual human sacrifice. And more alarming still was that these sacrifices were always non-believers or followers of other religions.

Was it possible this unsub thought Jimmy Loveridge was part of a rival fellowship, so took his life as a ritual sacrifice?

Ella searched for Santerians in Delaware but quickly found that the religion had been banned in certain parts of the world. North America was one of them. She widened her search before her phone distracted her.

That guy? Let me talk to him.

Ella re-read her previous message to decipher what the hell Mark was talking about. Then it hit her. He thought she was talking about Byford rather than the killer. She corrected herself.

Whoops, sorry! I was talking about our unsub, not my so-called partner. How are things at HQ? x

Ella scrolled through the pages, finding that the Santeria religion was still alive and well in underground circles. But how to get among them, that was the question. Apparently, followers of the religion kept their worshipping antics under wraps due to the legalities around the religion.

Another reply.

Don't call him your partner. What have you been doing together?

Ella read the message then threw her phone down in frustration. What was going through Mark's head to make him act like this? Where was the trust? You couldn't just blindly assume that your partner was going to sleep with the next person who came along. She wished she'd have seen this insecurity sooner because she would have had second thoughts about dating him. She left Mark on read. She didn't have time for this. Her unsub could be out there choosing his next time right this second, and she wasn't going to let a jealous partner get in the way of stopping him.

Something propelled her to get out of her seat. She needed a break from this room. Across the corridor, she spotted Sheriff Hunter walking into his office, so she headed his way.

"Sheriff," she said. "Could I use your skills a second?"

He slumped down in his chair and rubbed his face, the image of the classic overworked police officer.

"Sure. What's the situation? Any developments?"

"A few. I've found a small link between the victims, but I'm onto something much more interesting here."

"Oh?"

"Could you search the police database for something please? I don't have access to it."

"No problem." Hunter put on his glasses and logged on his computer. "What am I searching for?"

"Santeria," Ella said.

Hunter threw her a confused look. "What's that? Someone's name?"

"No, just a keyword. It's a long shot, I admit."

Hunter followed her request and typed it in. Ella corrected his spelling as he did. *SEARCHING...*

"Could take a while," Hunter said. "Not exactly hi-tech up in here. What's this word anyway?"

"It's an old religion," Ella said as she leaned over Hunter's desk, her eyes glued to the screen. "I'm running with the theory that these are some kind of sacrifices."

"Like, Satanic activity?" asked Hunter with a grimace.

"Something like that, but not quite. Something much more specific. It's a real religion and it has a deep connection to coins and human sacrifice. Maybe our unsub might be a devout follower."

"Nasty stuff, that. I lived through the Satanic panic in the eighties. It was a load of overblown rubbish if you ask me, but some crazies took it a bit too seriously. You still get the occasional criminal Satanist these days but they're…"

The screen pinged and interrupted Hunter's spiel. *0 RESULTS FOUND.*

"Damn, sorry girl. End of the line."

Ella cast her head back towards the ceiling. Disappointment again. "Like I said, it was a long shot. Thanks for trying." Ella headed back to the door.

"Hold up a second," the sheriff called. "You've got my mind whirring."

Ella spun around then held on to the doorframe, hoping the sheriff had a miracle up his sleeve. "I'm all ears."

"Santeria. I've heard that word before. Where have I heard it?"

Ella shrugged. "Could be a million places. It's banned in this country. Maybe something to do with that?"

Hunter threw his glasses on the table then tapped the back of his head against his chair. "No, no. There was a case a few years ago. I remember it because it reminded of that guitar player. Santana."

Hope sprung anew. Ella felt the rush. "A case involving Santeria? You're kidding?"

"No siree. Hold on. Let me work my magic." Hunter typed away, frustratingly slow. "There was a kid. Some grad student. He'd flipped a lid and tried to kill his professor."

"A kid? Like a teenager?"

"More like twenties. How old are kids in their last year of college? Twenty-one?"

"Yeah, more or less," she said.

Hunter's computer pinged. "Bam. Look who won the pony. Check this out." He waved his hand in excitement.

Ella rushed over and glared at the screen. 1 RESULT FOUND. Hunter clicked into the listing and up came a mugshot of an acne-ridden boy, dirty black hair covering his forehead. He had that dead-eye look, like he'd definitely stomped on a few small animals in his time.

"Holy cow. Who's this guy? What did he do?"

"This my friend is Daniel Garcia. Twenty-one years old, lives right here in Elsmere. This lunatic attacked his professor sometime last year, tried to kill him. We were called to the university to sort things out."

Ella scanned his file. He looked like a puny figure, someone easily able to sneak in and out of places without being seen. And it looked like he had a penchant for aggression too.

"He fits the profile, but what's this got to do with Santeria?" Ella asked.

The sheriff clicked onto the next page and scrolled through the notes. "There. The bottom section. Have a read of that."

Ella did, and couldn't quite believe what she was seeing.

"Oh… *damn.*"

"Told you."

A few seconds later, she was back in her office with car keys in hand.

***

During her rush to the car, she'd run into Byford outside the police precinct. She hadn't told him everything, just that they needed to check someone out pronto. Ella drove while Byford checked Daniel Garcia's profile on his phone.

"You'll have to explain this to me, Ella."

They got onto the Delaware streets. The GPS told her that the university was only five minutes away.

"You'll think I'm crazy, but hear me out."

Byford audibly sighed. "Alright."

Ella let it pass. No more arguments, she told herself. "I was looking into this ancient religion called Santeria. It's an old diasporic religion originally from Cuba but quickly moved all across the world. One of their traditions is human sacrifice which, get this, involves burying the dead with coins."

"Right. I'm following."

"I searched the police database and found nothing, but then the sheriff remembered a case from last year. This Garcia kid was an ancient studies major who had a violent outburst and attacked his professor."

"Okay," Byford shrugged, "but why?"

"Because the professor rejected his paper. And guess what his paper was on?"

"Oh, I see. Santeria."

"Exactly. And this guy fits the bill too. He's agile, has a history of violence and can't control his impulses. He's also pretty smart if he's a college kid."

Byford turned down the dial on the radio. "Well, I must say that's pretty good work. I'm impressed you got that so quickly. The problem I'm seeing here is that there's no address for this suspect."

"Yeah, I noticed that too. Hopefully the professor who got attacked will have some answers for us."

The university grounds came into view, occupying Ella's entire vision. She found the parking lot with some intense navigation and pulled in a space. The agents got out and walked across the grounds, coming across a statue in the form of a giant book. A young woman was sunbathing on it.

"Foyer, this way," Byford said. It had only been a few years since Ella had been to university but the whole establishment seemed alien to her now. Bodies swarmed past her, most glued to cell phones. Others sat around in groups on the vast and lush greenery. She felt a little uncomfortable here, like she was too old to be in such a place.

"Feels strange, doesn't it?" Byford said.

"You feel it too?"

"Oh yes. That's the generation gap at work. It only gets worse as you get older too."

Ella laughed. Finally, some personality. After what seemed like an endless walk, they reached the reception area. Ella buzzed for assistance and waited. Eventually, an older male rushed to the desk from a back room.

"Hello, sorry to keep you," he said. "How can I help?"

Ella held up her badge. "We're with the FBI. We're looking for a Professor Casey. Do you know where we can find him?"

The receptionist hadn't taken his eyes off Ella's badge, like she was showing him a picture of a gruesome medical experiment. "Umm, yes. I can get hold of him. Can I ask what this is about?"

"I'm afraid not. It's confidential."

"Okay, I'll just be a moment." The receptionist hurried into the back room. Ella used the opportunity to break open her new partner a little more.

"What university did you go to?" she asked.

Byford straightened his loose-fitting tie in the reflection of the reception window. "Illinois. I actually studied law."

Makes sense, Ella thought. He looked like a lawyer. "Wow, Illinois's a major one. The FBI is kind of a step down after that," she laughed.

"You could say that. The Bureau actually headhunted me. I couldn't say no. But sometimes I wish I had, given some of the things I've seen."

Ella wanted to ask more but the receptionist came back. "Professor Casey will be down in a moment," he said. "Would you like to take a seat while you wait?"

They did. Members of the student body came and went, casting them sly glances as they passed by. Ella knew they looked out of place but found it quite comforting that she did, in a way. She hadn't really liked her university years, and she was glad they were behind her, but she definitely missed the lack of responsibility.

"What kind of things did you see in counterterrorism?" she asked Byford, unable to resist the urge.

Byford tapped his foot against the marble floor. He bent sharply and cracked his neck. "Some things I'd like to erase," he said. "There's a reason I moved away from it, and it wasn't because of the pay."

"I've never had much interaction with that department. They're not even based in Washington, are they?"

"No, they're in the Chicago branch. That's where I was based. But I had to get away."

A man in a gray sweater and red trousers approached the reception window. He stuck his head underneath the glass. The receptionist pointed to the agents. This was him. Ella and Byford stood up to announce themselves.

"Hello, Professor Casey?" she asked, reaching out her hand. Casey took it with an unenthusiastic grip.

"Hi. Can I help you? You're with the FBI?"

He looked a timid soul. Very much on the short side with brief whispers of gray hair on his head. He had a faded goatee that resembled a style from a previous era.

"Sorry for the intrusion, but we'd like to talk to you about Daniel Garcia if you'd be willing."

Professor Casey's face fell flat when he heard the name. "Oh. You're here about that. I already told the police everything."

"This is something new," Ella said. "Garcia is a suspect in a new crime, and we were hoping you could help us track him down."

"Track him down? Well, I don't know about that. I just know I never want to see that kid again. Last I heard he was living with his mom. Her name's Elaine and lives somewhere in Elsmere. That's all I know."

Ella made her notes. "Thank you, professor. Do you have a moment to talk us through what happened?"

The professor checked his watch. "I really don't, I'm in a hurry. I can give you the short version but anything more will have to be done another time."

It was better than nothing, Ella thought. "Of course, we understand. The short version would be great."

"Daniel was a bright kid. Exceptionally bright, actually. He had incredible potential and I pushed him to utilize it. But he had a nasty streak to him. His home life wasn't perfect, and that came through in his work."

"I see," Ella said.

"For his final thesis, he wrote a paper on ancient mythology with a heavy focus on a particular part of it."

"Santeria, right?" Ella asked.

"Correct. Santeria. The paper was well-written and researched to exceptional levels, but it was..." Professor Casey scratched his head as he searched for the word. "Transgressive. Sensational. He wrote like a sympathizer of atrocities. I couldn't accept it, and when he found out I'd rejected him, he showed up after hours with a knife."

Ella and Byford exchanged a look. "He tried to stab you?"

Professor Casey nodded. "Yes. He aimed for my throat. I managed to skirt him, but it was difficult. Daniel is very agile. Very sneaky. He was expelled soon after."

"Did you press charges?" Byford asked.

"No. Daniel is a product of his home life. It's not his fault he grew up to be violent. The fact he found solace in this sinister faith is concerning and pressing charges against him would have angered him further. I was terrified he'd come back for me, so I didn't want to rattle the cage so to speak."

As far as Ella was concerned, they had everything they needed. This guy had some explaining to do. "Thank you so much professor. That's all I have to ask."

"I really must be running now, but if you need to know anything else, simply call the university."

The agents shook the man's hand and said their goodbyes. They headed back out the door, picking up speed as they did.

"Let's find this guy. Looks like we need to find an Elaine Garcia around here."

Ella had a good feeling about this. Something told her she needed to meet this young man. "My thoughts exactly. Let's find this guy."

CHAPTER TEN

Ella drove a little faster than she should have. According to the database, there was only one Elaine Garcia in the area. Sheriff Hunter texted over her address. It was a six-mile journey that Ella covered in half the time it should have taken.

"Jesus, this place is… something," Ella said.

The street consisted of one tight road and two rows of houses. On one of the fences, the homeowner had hung out their dirty washing for everyone to see. One of the houses didn't have a front door, just a hole where it should be.

"Are we in the right place?" asked Byford. "I hate to generalize but I can't see a kid around here going to college."

"College is cheap until you leave," Ella said.

"I suppose. Here," Byford pointed. "Number nineteen."

Ella pulled up on the curb outside the home. It had a small porch, tattered to ruin, and a flight of steps that looked on the verge of collapse. The whole house was painted a charcoal gray that did nothing to disguise the waning exterior. Across the street, a young kid on a bike observed their intrusion.

Ella gave three knocks on the door. A dog began yapping on the other side before she'd even finished. Then came the sound of human life on the other side. A woman's face appeared between the cracks, but Ella couldn't make out much about her.

"Hi, Elaine Garcia?"

The woman sniffed loudly. "Who's asking?"

"The FBI. I'm Agent Dark and this is Agent Byford…"

"FBI?" she shouted with a piercing shrill. "What gives you the right to come here?"

"We're here to speak with your son," Byford added.

"You'll need to tell me more than that, pal. I got six of them."

"Daniel Garcia," Ella said. "Is he home?"

"Danny don't live here no more," Elaine said and shut the door. Ella had it scouted. She thrust her foot in the door gap.

"Well, could you tell us where he is?"

Elaine looked down at Ella's foot like it was an artifact from another planet. She pushed the door against it harder to keep her out. It was only a moderate amount of pain, but it brought the adrenaline to the surface.

"These boots weren't made for walking, Mrs. Garcia. Please tell us where your son is."

Elaine relieved the pressure and opened the door up. She glanced between like the agents like she was waiting for them to make the first move. "I don't know where he is. That little runt could be anywhere by now."

"How do you mean? We were under the impression he lived with you."

"What's this about? What's he done now?"

"We can't say. It's confidential. But if you help us find him, then we might be able to give you the details."

"And how am I supposed to do that? You want me to whistle for him?" Elaine said.

"Don't you have his phone number?" asked Byford. "Seems unlikely that you wouldn't."

"Danny upped and left after his little fight last year. I haven't seen the dickhead since. Okay?" She tried to slam the door again, but Ella's foot was still lodged in place. "You wanna leave me alone now? I can't help you."

Elaine's tone didn't sit right with Ella. There were cracks in her voice, like she was reluctant to spill the words she did. If Mia was here, she'd say it was a telltale sign of lying. Ella decided to go for broke.

"Mrs. Garcia, forgive me for being blunt, but I think you're lying to us."

The comment enlivened something in the woman. "Lying? Who are you to tell me I'm lying you little bitch?" The door swung open, and Elaine lunged outside. Byford jumped between them and held Elaine back.

"You want to get arrested?" he asked, "because that's what happens when you assault an agent."

"I don't really give a shit," shouted Elaine. Ella turned around to see a few bystanders watching from their doorsteps. Then, she spotted the boy on the bike. He had his arm outstretched, pointing at something beside Elaine's house.

"Danny!" the kid shouted.

Ella followed the kid's pointing and saw a man, dressed entirely in black, slyly stepping over the garden wall. She couldn't see his face, but she didn't need to.

"That's him," she called as she struck Byford on the arm. "He's here."

The man in black froze when he heard his name, turned towards the agents then sped off down the street. His feet clattered thunderously as his outline gradually got smaller, but Ella was fast in pursuit. She leaped over the wall, took off down the road and didn't stop to look back.

"Daniel," she shouted as loudly as her lungs allowed. "FBI. Stop."

The suspect didn't obey, or maybe didn't even hear. The rows of houses passed by in a blur as she turned a corner, finding herself standing in front of a small park. A large grassy area surrounded it, but more alarmingly, there was no sign of Daniel. Byford appeared beside her, breathless.

"Where'd he go?"

"Don't know. He can't have gone far. I knew she was lying to us."

"Where would you go if you were him?" Byford said. "Think. You can get in his head."

Ella tried but the adrenaline was making it hard to think straight. The park was deserted so any moving figures would immediately jump out. There were none.

This guy was fast and agile, but tactful too. If he could get into people's homes unnoticed, that meant he could hide himself well. Ella scanned every piece of apparatus in the park. A swing, climbing frame, tunnel, roundabout. Very small with no signs of intrusion. Even the gate was shut.

The spring wind blew against her face. It rustled the leaves of the trees up above. She leaned against the nearest tree to regain her strength, and as she did, she noticed a few scratches in the bark.

She followed the pattern upwards. More marks.

Then a muddy footprint.

Ella took a few steps back and looked towards the sky. Something unnatural sat among nature.

"Byford, up there!" she shouted. He followed her eye line and landed on the same thing she did. He drew his pistol and aimed it skyward.

"Daniel, you're not getting out of here. Come down immediately."

Nestled between the thick cluster of branches was a man dressed in a black hoodie, his face concealed. He hunched over, like an animal on the cusp of hibernation.

"Daniel, we just want to talk to you," she shouted. "There's no escape now, so you may as well give it up."

"I didn't mean to do it," a voice called down. "It was an accident."

"What was an accident, Daniel?" said Byford.

"All of it. I have problems. You can't help me."

"No we can't, but we can arrest you," said Byford. "If you don't come down in five seconds, I'm going to fire a warning shot, understand?"

Something seemed off. A killer like this wouldn't confess so willingly. They would fight until their bodies gave out.

"Daniel, what are you talking about? Are you saying you killed two people by accident?"

Daniel's hood fell down and revealed his face for the first time. His unwashed hair hung down to his chin and outlined his skinny features like a dirty picture frame.

"Killed people?" he called. The branches rustled again as he adjusted. "No."

"Then what do you mean?" Ella called.

Byford interjected. "Daniel, I'm counting down. Five, four…"

Ella leaned in to him and whispered. "Stop. He's coming round. No warning shots needed."

Byford didn't listen. "Three…"

"I didn't do nothing," Daniel said again, more desperation in his voice.

"Nigel, seriously. Just wait. He can't stay up there forever. A warning shot is just going to put up his defenses," said Ella. She directed her voice at the suspect again. "Daniel, we promise we just want to talk to you."

"Don't shoot me. I haven't done anything wrong."

"Two….one…." Byford finished.

"Dan, I just want to talk to you about Santeria. Okay? That's all."

The suspect turned and looked at his aggressors for the first time, but the brief moment of connectivity was suddenly dashed. A deafening gun blast shattered the eardrums of everyone in the vicinity, juddering the tree branches as though they were being shaken by a giant.

"No! What the hell are you doing?" Ella screamed as she grabbed Nigel's wrist. The ringing in her head drowned out the sound of her own voice.

The next thing she saw, in some surreal slow motion, was Daniel Garcia's body fall from the trees.

CHAPTER ELEVEN

Mia tracked the license plate and followed it a few miles outside of Manhattan. In the passenger seat beside her, Melissa fiddled with the radio dials to the point of irritation.

"Just leave it on one station," Mia said.

"Sorry. I didn't like that song."

"Focus on the task at hand. They're right up ahead."

Fingerprints from the Manhattan crime scene had revealed two potential perpetrators. A couple of local boys named Billy and Patrick, rumored to be part of a criminal gang according to local police. Mia tailed the black SUV up a country lane, being sure to keep a discreet amount of distance.

"They're going into the gas station," Melissa said, her voice trembling. Mia recognized that tone. It was the tone of reality hitting home.

"Yes, and we're going there too."

"What? We're arresting them? Right here?"

"We're talking to them. That's all. We have their names, license plates, and their addresses. If they get away, we can still find them. We're not dragging them kicking and screaming."

Melissa gripped the arm of the passenger door. "But they're massive. You saw the size of them, right?"

Mia watched the black SUV pull up to the pump at the far end of the forecourt. She took the one at the back. She saw the silhouettes of her suspects move back and forth in the wing mirror.

"Right, how comfortable are you with this?" Mia asked. "I know this is nerve-wracking but it's part of the job."

Melissa shook her head. "I don't know. I'm worried. This all seems a bit real now."

"Oh yeah, that'll happen. Get used to it. I tell you what, I'll go talk to him on my own. You stay here and observe. Okay?"

Melissa agreed. "Done. I'll be your backup."

Mia removed her gun from her holster and placed it in the glove box. "I don't need to tell you *not* to touch this, right? For obvious reasons."

"Of course."

From the same compartment, Mia pulled out an electronic taser. "You see this? Taser. It has a thirty-foot radius, so you can shoot a bitch from two streets away, okay?"

Melissa took the taser and inspected it. "I know. I've used a taser before."

"Good. Stay alert. Have handcuffs prepped too, just in case."

Mia exited the car with eyes locked on her suspect. He was a large, well-built gentleman in a vest and jeans. His head was completely shaved, reflecting the afternoon sunlight off his enormous skull. He had a pump in hand.

"Excuse me," Mia said, gripping her own taser in her pocket. "Are you Billy Graham?"

The gentleman eyed her with great suspicion. "Yeah. I am." The gas pump fizzled to life as he began filling his SUV with diesel.

"My name's Agent Ripley. I'm with the FBI. Could we talk for a moment?" She saw Billy clench his fist. Usually, suspects emitted a note of concern when she announced herself as the FBI. Billy didn't seem fazed by it.

"Talking now, aren't we?" he said. He took his hands off the pump and let the auto-fill function do the rest.

"Could you tell me where you were at midnight last night?"

"Let me think. I was down the bar."

"Which one?"

"One in town. Can't remember the name. Sixteen beers will do that to you."

"I see. In that case, could you tell me why your fingerprints were found at a crime scene this morning? A young banker by the name of Tony Atlas. Recognize the name?"

Billy turned his back to her for a second as he messed with the pump. "Don't know what you're talking about sweetheart. Never heard that name before."

"Strange. Because your brother's prints were found in there too. Why would you both pay a visit to an investment banker at midnight?"

"Buying weed. End of," Billy grunted.

"So you *do* know him? Why did you say you didn't?"

"You need to leave us well alone," Billy said, still with his back to Mia. "This is nothing to do with you or anyone else."

"Homicide definitely *is* something to do with me. Do you want to start telling me the…"

Billy cut Mia's sentence off with a sudden lunge in her direction. In a single millisecond, his bulky hands were reaching towards her neck. Mia was ready for the attack. She grabbed both his wrists and kicked him between the legs. Billy fell back, only momentarily dazed, then started towards Mia again.

A second later, he was on her. Her legs gave way and she toppled to the ground, this hulking beast on top of her. He pulled his fist backward and struck down against her forehead, knocking all of the cognitive abilities right out of her skull. Then the man's hands were at her neck, and all Mia could do was kick her legs against his rock-solid lower body. It didn't do much to subdue him, only angered him further.

Mia saw the sky turn a little darker, then realized it was her own consciousness fading. She felt for her taser but couldn't get a grip on it. She just needed a little leverage. In her dreary state, her muscle memory recalled a neat little maneuver. Mia once referred to it as a Muay Thai, but her teacher always corrected her. It was actually *bujinkan*.

She clutched her knees around her attacker and arched her back as much as she could. She pressed her thighs against the man's ribs and did everything in her power to roll forward just an inch. Billy fell back for a flash, and that was all Mia needed to strike. Her hand found the taser, withdrew it and shot Billy clean in the chest. His body failed him, and he toppled backward like a falling tower, ripping the diesel pump out of the vehicle and spilling fuel onto the ground. Mia felt it gush against her ankles, but the burning sensation brought her back to the present.

Billy gasped for breath on the ground while Mia rushed to cuff the man. She had him face down when another soul made itself known in her peripheral vision. Billy's passenger had climbed out to see the action up close, but the look on his face said he wanted no part of this. He ran off down the lane, passing by Mia's car as he did.

"Melissa!" Mia shouted. "Get him."

Her partner slowly stepped out of the car, much to Mia's frustration. Melissa watched the escapee disappear down the way. "Cuff this idiot and get him in the car. Now! I'm going after the other one."

Melissa jogged over and did what she had to, trembling the entire time. Mia heard the cuffs clink and that was enough to put her mind at rest. Billy would be out for at least a few minutes. More than enough time to get him locked in the vehicle.

Mia took off down the lane, taser in hand. She saw the escapee's figure about thirty feet down the road. She continued on for a few seconds, aimed with her taser, fired and missed. The man was unrelenting in his mission to escape, gradually diminishing from view.

What to do? Chase him? Call it a success? One suspect was better than no suspects.

Then from the other direction, Mia heard a scream. She ran back to the gas station and saw Melissa lying on the forecourt floor clutching her nose. Beyond that, Billy Graham was escaping in the opposite direction.

"Shit," she shouted. In the blink of an eye, Melissa had scrambled to her feet and pulled something out of the passenger side of the car.

No, don't you dare, Mia thought. It all happened too fast to get her words out properly.

"Melissa, put that fucking thing down! Do *not* shoot that gun!"

Billy Graham passed by his car and up the hill. How he regained composure so quickly was unlike anything Mia had seen before.

"He's getting away," Melissa screamed. She leaned against the hood of the car, aimed the pistol towards the fading suspect.

"The fumes," Mia shouted. "The Goddamn fumes."

Melissa, slack against the car, fired the pistol. Mia's instinct was to drop to her floor, but instead, she hurled herself towards her partner as fast her joints would take her.

But it was too late. She first heard the bullet hit the car up ahead. The clink of metal on metal. Then came the fireworks. Billy's car exploded like a miniature volcano erupting for the first time in a thousand years. A gigantic cloud of black smoke surged into the afternoon sky, and for a second Mia wondered if this was the end.

Mia grabbed Melissa's hand and pulled her away from the scene. "Why? For Christ's sakes, why would you do that?" she screamed at her.

Melissa's eyes were frozen in a look of abject dread. Up by the flaming car, a bunch of gas station attendees appeared with fire extinguishers. They squirted foam onto the burning vehicle, risking their lives in the process. Another one, a young woman, ran over to the agents. Melissa immediately hugged the woman.

"Are you hurt? Do you need an ambulance?" the woman asked, furiously glancing between the two agents.

Mia wasn't quite sure what to make of all this. Were they hurt? She wouldn't know until the adrenaline wore off.

"We're fine. Are you guys okay? Was anyone else hurt?" Mia asked.

"No. There's no one else here. Just the staff. What the hell was that about?"

"We're FBI. Maybe former FBI now. Please, this was an... accident."

"No shit," the woman said. "Don't worry, fire brigade is on the way."

"Tell those guys to get away from that car. What if the fumes ignite? This place could blow."

The woman shook her head. "Diesel fumes don't catch fire. Plus, I switched off the supply. It's fine."

Melissa dropped to the floor, still glued to the now-smoking rubble. "I... I can't believe that."

Mia backed away and surveyed the scene, her vision clouded with fury. She suddenly thought of the escaped suspects, but there were more important things to worry about now, like how she'd explain this to FBI officials. Melissa was a rookie and it was Mia's responsibility to keep her behavior in check, but this wasn't just a rookie mistake. Back at the suicide victim's apartment, Melissa acted as any trainee would. It was understandable, even expected.

But this was a catastrophic error that could have resulted in mass death. Melissa had fired at a fleeing suspect, which would be difficult to justify but not impossible. But firing while gas leaked all over the garage forecourt?

This could be the thing that brought Mia's thirty-year career to an end.

Maybe it was time, Mia thought as she tugged on her ponytail. Had she not explained herself properly to her new partner? Was it all her fault for not being clear?

The flaming wreckage became a thick tornado of black smoke, the risk of explosion dissolving into the sky. In the distance, she heard the fire engine sirens. They needed to get back to HQ and get their punishments over and done with, the idea of which brought another bout of rage.

Mia didn't know if she had it in her anymore.

CHAPTER TWELVE

"Daniel," Ella shouted and ran towards the body at the foot of the tree. She shook him, rolled him over and then tapped his cheeks. "Byford, what the hell is wrong with you? He could have fallen and broken his spine."

"It was a warning shot. And we need to arrest him. He's a suspect. We can't just *talk* to him."

There was no blood, but Daniel was unresponsive. The blast must have shocked the boy to the point he lost control. She checked his pulse. "He's alive. No thanks to you."

At her touch of his wrist, Daniel stirred on the ground. Ella released him as he slowly climbed to his knees.

"The fuck happened there? I was out cold. Where am I?"

The agents stayed quiet as Daniel came around. He sat with his back against the tree and blinked himself back to full consciousness. When he saw the agents in front of him, the fury came back. He tried to rise to his feet but didn't have the strength.

"You two. Shit, I thought I dreamt that. What do you want from me?"

"Daniel, we just want to talk, okay? We're not accusing you of anything. Do you feel alright?"

"Get rid of the asshole, then me and you talk," Daniel said. He directed his venom at Byford. "He goes."

"I'm sorry, but we have to take you into custody," Byford said. "You're a suspect in a murder investigation."

"No I'm not!" Daniel shouted. The force pulled a nerve somewhere in his spine. He grabbed it and moaned in pain. "Shit, that hurts."

Ella turned to her partner and did her best to conceal her exasperation. Byford wasn't rolling with her at all on this. Daniel was at the center of the rope, and they were both pulling on different ends, but she couldn't show irritation in front of a suspect. She'd have to deal with Byford in a more private arena.

"Nigel, trust me on this. Just do what he asks."

"Do what he asks?" he laughed. "This man could have killed two people. We have an obligation to take him in."

Ella didn't want to do that. In an interrogation room, Daniel wouldn't be his real self. Out here, he would tell the truth. And there was something about him that seemed a little off to her. Right now, she didn't think Daniel was the person responsible for the recent murders. He had a macabre side to him, and he was certainly guilty of something, but whether it was murder or not was another question.

Ella lowered her voice to a whisper. "I got us this far and I'm going to get us further. Just wait around the corner. If he runs, I'll call you. At that point we take him in."

Nigel rubbed his temples in a display of frustration. "Fine. Do whatever you want." He took one last look at the suspect and walked off back towards the street. *Just what I need*, she thought, *another problem to deal with*. If Mia was here, she'd have caught Ella's vibe, rolled with it and changed tactics if it didn't work. Byford worked by the book, and if there was something Ella had learned in her short career, it was that protocol wasn't always gospel.

Once he was out of earshot, Ella offered Daniel some assistance.

"Want a hand getting up?"

Daniel took a moment. "Okay." He reached out his hand. Ella took it and hauled him from his sitting position to his feet. She held his shoulders to steady him.

"Feel alright?"

"Yeah, thanks. That fall though."

"It looked pretty bad. I'm sorry. I didn't want it to happen like that."

"Your partner's a douchebag," Daniel said as he pushed his hair off his face. He let go of Ella and composed himself. He checked his balance by walking on his tiptoes.

"So, I helped you. You have to help me. I need you to be honest with me, alright?"

"I'm being honest. I don't know what you're talking about."

"Want to tell me what happened with you and your professor last year?"

Daniel leaned against the tree and adjusted his hoodie. He pulled his jeans up and checked the contents of his pockets. "I had an episode. That's it."

"An episode?"

"Yeah. A manic episode. I worked my ass off on that project and he just told me it sucked. That's what triggered it."

"So your response was to attack him? That isn't normal behavior, even for a manic episode," Ella said. "Be honest with me."

Daniel covered his mouth with his hand and breathed through the cracks in his fingers. "Okay. You want honesty? I wanted to kill him like the Santerians would have. Happy? That's why I hauled ass when you knocked on my door. I heard the guy's name and it just... triggered everything. I thought the professor had gone to the cops to press charges or whatever."

There it was. Ella felt the sincerity of every syllable. His inflection changed. His tone was a little more relaxed. The sound of truth.

"But why? Why did you want to kill Professor Cole? Because of a bad grade?"

"Not a bad grade. A total rejection. And you gotta understand, I'd been reading about that shit for years. It was my escape from my shitty life. Some of it got lodged in my brain, alright? I thought killing the professor would be some kind of... I don't know... poetic justice."

"And you don't follow the religion anymore?" asked Ella.

"Follow it? Hell no. I never believed any of it. It was cool, but it was obviously all bullshit."

Ella felt the sincerity again. She watched his body language closely and saw no emotional or mental barriers in place. He genuinely didn't follow the religion, and perhaps never did. The chances of him being this killer were looking less likely by the second.

"Are you aware there were two recent murders, both of which looked like something straight from a Santerian execution?"

"What?" Daniel asked. "Murders? Santerian? You gotta be shitting me."

"I'm not. We have two men, both discovered dead in their homes with coins around their eyes."

The suspect's bottom lip began to quiver. In some people, that was a sign of guilt or an incoming confession. But Daniel kept his cool. "That's insane. How were they killed?"

"Throats were slashed."

"Crap. Well, that's nasty, but I had nothing to do with it. Swear on my life."

"You understand how much of a coincidence this is?" Ella asked. Right now, she was three-quarters sure Daniel wasn't her man, but she needed evidence to take it to a whole. "A Santerian obsessive living a few miles from these murders. It's hard for us to look past."

Daniel began to pace. If he ran in the next few seconds, he was guilty. Ella kept a close eye on the direction his feet were facing.

"When were they killed?"

"April 27 and April 30. Sometime around one in the morning."

Daniel backed up against the tree again. He looked back over the trees towards his house. "Last week?"

"Yes."

"It couldn't have been me. I was at my dad's house in Greensboro. Me and all my brothers."

"Really? You can verify that?" Greensboro was about three states away. Not impossible to get back from, but unlikely, Ella thought.

Daniel clenched his fist in success. "Yes! I still got my bus ticket too. Ask anyone. Dad, brothers, uncle. We even have some videos from the week."

"We'll need to see them, okay? It's not that I don't believe you, but we need evidence to exclude you."

"I get it. I'll show you everything."

"We'll send an officer to your home to get them. Please tell your mom to expect him," Ella said. She felt a twinge of disappointment that she'd come so close only to reach a dead end, but in another way, she was glad that Daniel wasn't her culprit. He seemed to be a lost soul still searching for his place in the world. She felt sympathy for him, not pity or disgust. She would probably never see him again, but she didn't want to see his potential go to waste.

"Yeah, she's a bitch sometimes. Can you show me any crime scene photos?" he asked.

Ella couldn't quite believe his boldness. "Afraid not. That's confidential."

Daniel stuffed his hands in his pockets. He bent his shoulder back and it cracked loudly. "Ouch. Well, can I just ask one question?"

"Go ahead."

"You said you found the coins in the guys' eyes right?"

"Yes."

"Heads or tails?"

"Very funny."

"No, I mean it. Which side was showing outwards?"

Now that Ella thought about it, she didn't know. That wasn't something she thought was necessary, but now that Daniel mentioned it, it could be an important factor. "Damn, I don't actually know. Let me check."

She pulled out her phone, swiping away a few messages from Mark in the process. She pulled up the crime scene photo she needed.

"Heads."

"Aha. Well, you need to research better, because Santerians don't show heads."

Ella couldn't quite believe she hadn't taken that part into account. It was probably crucial to his ritual. She silently cursed herself. "They don't?"

"Nu-huh. When they make sacrifices, it's always the tail side that faces outward. It's symbolic. They want the hounds of hell constantly chasing their sacrifices in the afterlife. The demons of hell chase your tail, you see?"

"Oh, damn. I didn't know that. Thank you for clearing that up." That changed everything, Ella thought. Maybe she'd been on a wrong path from the start with this theory. And to think that poor Daniel was almost killed because of her ideas. Shame knotted up her stomach like a coiled snake and for a second, she couldn't look the boy in the eye. She was ready to scratch off everything and start again from new, as much as it would hurt to do so.

"Yeah, and throat slitting? Another no-no. Santerians cut their victims through the heart. Never anything else."

Another blow, but by now, a welcome one. Ella needed to get back and collect her thoughts. "Thank you, Daniel. You've been a great help, and I'm sorry about my partner. Shall we head back?"

They began walking back from where they came. "Sure. Don't worry about your partner. Shit happens. I'll be around when the cops come. And good luck with everything."

"You too. And please, go back and finish your studies when you're allowed. Don't waste it."

"Ha. Can't afford it. You've seen where I live, right? I had a scholarship and blew it. Lost my shit, lost my scholarship. Simple as."

"Go to another school. I grew up in a dive too, but my studies got me out of there. You don't have to be a prisoner of your past." Ella spotted Byford waiting in their cruiser at the edge of the road. "Here's my ride. We'll be in touch shortly."

Daniel waved bye and walked past towards his home, ignoring Byford in the vehicle. Ella got in.

"Back to square one," she said. "Come on, I'm ready to rest."

CHAPTER THIRTEEN

Ella checked into the motel two streets away from the precinct. The clerk behind the desk handed her a key and told her that breakfast was served between six and nine. Byford was still at the precinct finishing some things off, but she'd hit a wall for the day. She could think no more, so decided it was time to get some rest.

She took the stairs for the exercise, noting the rich mahogany banisters on her way up. The motel was only a two-story building, probably with around fifty rooms in total. So far, she hadn't seen another soul, only a clerk and a parking assistant. When she came to her floor, she felt her phone vibrate in her pocket, already knowing what name was flashing on her screen. Since she hadn't replied to his last message, he'd sent her more messages than she thought possible. She'd only been away for a day, and he was already on her like a greyhound on a rabbit. It was all getting a bit much, even at this early stage.

Ella swiped her keycard in the door and entered her living quarters for the foreseeable future. She had a single bed, a nightstand, and a TV angled in the high corner of the wall. There were some questionable style decisions dotted around, particularly the red and yellow drapes, but she didn't plan on spending a whole lot of time here anyway. Starting tomorrow, she had to crack this thing open. She had the knowledge and the skills to do it; she just needed to apply it.

She floored her bags then sat on the bed. Again, her phone buzzed, and only now she realized she'd been buzzed so much she'd lost feeling in that part of her leg. She grabbed the phone from her pocket.

Where are you?

Mark again. No kisses. No well-wishes. Or was it just his writing style? They said that around seventy percent of all text-based communication was misinterpreted. Maybe she was in the majority without realizing it.

She pulled up her contacts and hit Mark's name. She wasn't going to spend her night going back and forth with him like this. She had thinking to do.

It dialed. One ring. Mark picked up before the second ring.

71

"Finally."

"Hello to you too," she said.

"Never mind hello. I texted you about three hours ago."

He didn't sound like the same person. There was a venomous tone to his voice. Was he drunk or something?

"Mr. Balzano, I'm working a murder investigation in case you forgot. I've been working my socks off. Delaware's a hectic place."

"You couldn't find five seconds to reply to me?"

The volume of his voice rose. It crackled down the line. She could hardly believe he was talking to her like this.

"Mark, it's been non-stop. I've been on the road, interviewing people, hunting down a suspect. Most of the time I didn't even have my phone with me. What's gotten into you?"

"Nothing's gotten into me. I just want to know you're safe. Am I the asshole for wanting my girlfriend to be safe?"

They hadn't used the girlfriend or boyfriend word yet. It was a conversation they were yet to have, and it had been so long since Ella had a boyfriend that she couldn't remember how those conversations went. Or were they just brushed past these days? Modern relationships had so many designations that she wasn't even sure what they were classified as. Life partner, exclusive partner, friend with benefits? Definitely not the last one, she thought. Right now, it didn't seem like being with Mark had many benefits.

"Not at all. I love that you care about me. But you need to accept that I have responsibilities too. I can't just drop everything to text my…" she hesitated at the word. Somehow, it didn't seem right calling him it. It felt too permanent, too committed. But she did it anyway, prioritizing his feelings over her concern. "Boyfriend," she finished.

"Right. I get it. Your first boyfriend in forever and you can't make time for me? I've been worried sick. What if you were dead?"

Ella moved the phone away from her ear and took a deep breath. She felt like she was trying to sneak past a sleeping baby on a floor made of explosives. "Dead? You have that little faith in me?"

"You could be. How am I supposed to know if you don't text me?"

"So what, I'm supposed to text you every minute to tell you I'm alive? That's ridiculous and you know it."

"Right, now I'm ridiculous. If this is how you treat your boyfriends, no wonder you've been single for so long."

Mark had launched a poison dart and was waiting for it to take effect. Ella got up and opened the window. Suddenly the room felt suffocating. "I was single because I wanted to be, actually. Sometimes relationships don't seem worth the hassle."

"Is that a dig?" Mark asked. "What are you trying to say?"

Ella stuck her head out the window and breathed in fresh air. It cleared her head enough to realize that this conversation was only going one way.

"I'm just trying to say that jealousy will get us nowhere. Look, I'm with you, okay? Not anyone else. Not Byford, not Roy in accounting, not John Cena. I chose you, so cool it with the insecurity." Maybe a joke would calm him down. It didn't seem to do the trick.

"This is funny to you, huh?"

"No, it isn't, but our jobs are going to keep us apart occasionally. You'll be back out in the field soon too. What happens then? Are we gonna stay on the phone constantly?"

"We'll message. Like I've been trying to today."

Ella sat on the edge of the bed and looked down at the still life below. Not a soul moved. Orange streetlamps lined the street like sentries.

"Yeah, we will, when we have time. Besides, too much talking and you'll get sick of me." Ella slammed the window shut because it was getting a little cold in the room.

Mark stopped talking for a second. She wondered if the line had cut out by accident. Would that even be a bad thing?

"Send me a picture," he demanded, his booming voice startling her.

Ella panicked a little. Was this that sexting thing that Jenna always talked about? If so, she wasn't in the mood. Plus, it sounded like something more awkward than enjoyable. "A picture? Of what?"

Please don't say what I think you're going to say.

"Of you. In your room."

"Umm, okay. Can I ask why?"

"Because I just heard a noise."

Ella looked around. She could see every square inch of the room and hadn't heard a noise. "Huh? You think someone's trying to break in my room?"

"No, and stop making jokes. I think someone else is in your room with you. Something banged. Who else is there?"

Ella replayed the last few seconds in her mind. Then she remembered. "That was the window, doofus. I shut it."

"Send me a picture and make it quick. And send me the confirmation of your motel booking. I want to know you and this new partner are in separate rooms."

This must be some kind of joke, Ella thought. There was no way in hell Mark was being serious.

"Mark, what the hell…" she said before she realized she was talking to a dead phone line. No, he was being deadly serious by the sound of it. Of all the things to mess with her head tonight, she never expected it to be her own boyfriend.

Now that she was off the phone, she quickly realized how absurd this all was. She felt more alone than when she was single and felt like she'd transitioned into a human punching bag. He couldn't treat her like a child, nor like an obedient slave.

There'd be no pictures. No videos. No constant check-ins. Mark would have to live in the same reality as her, not some fantasy world where she played the part of his servant.

When she got back to D.C., she needed to have a difficult conversation.

***

In her dream, she was trapped in a cold prison cell. Not a modern one like she'd seen in Maine Correctional, but an old, rusty cage with iron bars and giant padlocks and gray walls. In the cell opposite her, another woman sat cradling herself, rocking back and forth. They were both wearing baggy white overalls with numbers on the front. Ella was 13, her new friend was 12.

Ella pushed her face against the bars. "What's wrong?" she asked the inmate. Upon closer inspection, she realized the woman was crying.

"It's my day."

"Your day?"

"May 2nd at 7am. It's the day they take me."

"Who? Who takes you?"

The woman pushed her scraggly brown hair back and showed her face. Ella didn't recognize her. "Them. The sands of time are running low."

Footsteps sounded beside them and a figure in black appeared between the two cages. The hooded man stood with his back to Ella, speaking Bible verses to the woman on the other side. Ella heard the word *amen,* then the figure vanished as quickly as he arrived.

"It's my time to go now," the woman said, wiping away tears. "If you get out, tell my boy I'll miss him. Tell him I'm sorry I made a mistake."

Two guards arrived, both faceless. One unlocked the woman's cell, took her hand and brought her to her feet. "Time to go, ma'am," he said. Ella reached out to grab the woman and hold her back, maybe giving her precious more seconds to live. But even though her hand connected with the shabby cloth, she found she had no strength or grip in this strange world.

They disappeared into the blackness of the corridor, floor creaking with every step. When silenced resumed, it was broken by the sound of laughter. She couldn't see another soul, but she could hear one. Keys jangled, then a prison jailer manifested from the darkness. He tapped his keys against the bars, dangling them in front of Ella like food to a starving animal. This time, she recognized the face.

"Mark," she said. "It's you."

"Yes, it's me. Who did you think it was?"

"What's going on? What am I doing here?" Ella cried.

"Look out the window."

Ella turned to the back wall, only now noticing a small rectangular pane of glass behind the bars. She pushed her face as close as she could to it. Outside, on a long stretch of grass, stood the gallows. Two guards pushed Ella's new friend towards it, all while she tried to escape their clutches. She couldn't, and once she was on the platform, she seemed to accept her fate.

Ella turned back to the jailer. "When's my turn?" she said. "I'm next in line."

Mark threw his head back and laughed again. "Good one. Sorry, Agent Dark, but the noose is too good for you. I'm afraid you're staying in here forever," he said as he vanished back into the darkness. In her immobile dream state, Ella couldn't respond, only accept the punishment. She turned back to the window to see the woman, now with a bag over her head, wait inertly for her fate to come.

And amazingly, Ella envied the woman.

BANG.

She heard the drop worlds away in her own reality. Her body jerked, and she suddenly woke up in a motel bed somewhere in Delaware. The relief came in a heavy wave. She wasn't in a nineteenth-century prison cell. She was free. No one had been hanged.

"Christ," she said aloud, catching her breath. Why did it feel so real? It was only a nightmare.

She heard the bang again, the same one as when the gallows trapdoor opened. She wondered for a second if she wasn't still in a dream world, but confirmed she wasn't when she saw her earthly

75

belongings. Her bag, her pistol, those red and yellow drapes. Something here was making a noise, and this time, it wasn't the window.

Ella stepped out of bed, finding her room freezing cold. She hurried into the bathroom and checked for any leaks, or maybe an adventurous mouse. She switched the light on and saw nothing living. Just a toilet, bath, sink and empty trash can.

Back in the main room, she switched on the lamp and moved to the door. She had sudden déjà vu from her last case. She peered through the peephole out into the dim corridor, waiting for her vision to adjust to the darkness.

When it did, she felt her body go numb. Someone stared back at her. A figure was standing right outside her door.

Midnight adrenaline started up, and Ella ran back and grabbed her pistol off the nightstand. Her hand was on the doorknob a second later, and she pulled it open and stepped out in one swift movement. She aimed her pistol in one direction, then jerked the other way.

Just empty space.

She didn't dream this. She couldn't have. Two eyeballs stared at her when she looked through that peephole. She would bet her life on it.

Then why didn't she hear them run? Where were they now?

In the long corridor, Ella felt as exposed as she could possibly be. There were places for people to hide along here. She'd be safer in her room.

She retreated back but stopped when she saw something that wasn't there before.

A piece of paper had been stuck on the door. An envelope. Ella gripped her pistol and did one last scan of the area. When she was confident no one was around, she tore the envelope off the door and went back inside her room.

The envelope was blank but unsealed. She pulled open the tab, reached in and unfolded a piece of writing paper.

When she saw the words, she suddenly envied the hanging woman again.

You didn't think I'd forgotten about you, did you?

CHAPTER FOURTEEN

This one was going to be a little harder than the others, he realized. There were no easy entry points, no isolated areas to take cover in. It was one am, so the rabble were asleep, but that just meant his activities were the only sounds to potentially wake up curious neighbors. The house was detached so he could sneak around the sides but doing so still came with great risk.

It had been a long time since he'd been here. He could hardly believe the old man still lived in this place. He must really love this town.

But what a fool, the old man. That just meant finding him was much easier than he thought.

He checked the houses for any lights and saw only one at the far end of the row. He slipped down the side of the old man's house and found the only thing blocking his exit to the garden was an iron gate. He gently shook it to ensure it wasn't loose, then used the handle as a foothold to launch himself over it. He cleared it in one movement, hitting the lawn feet-first on the other side. Barely a sound was made in the process.

He hid under the cover of the brick wall, peering around to see a glass door leading into the lounge. A new addition, the man thought. It didn't look like this years ago.

The TV was on, some old film by the looks of it, flashing the room shades of gray. Opposite the TV, the old man lay on the couch beneath a blanket. Given his age, probably long asleep by now.

The door handle rejected his intrusion. Locked. But seeing this garden now, although it was much different than he remembered, brought back an abundance of familiarities. He'd stand around in here while the men did business inside, wandering around, kicking dirt and climbing on the old man's statues. He never thought he'd see this part of the town again, or even wanted to, but under these circumstances, it was more than acceptable.

Then he remembered that little place the old man called his den.

With his head down and hood up, he hurried past the window to the other side of the garden. Muscle memory brought it all back in seconds. Leading down below the kitchen was a very thin set of stairs, down to the zone where this once-young man feared to tread. It was a tight squeeze, and there was a metal trash container at the bottom; he skirted around it without breaking the silence of the night.

The looming red door was his obstacle, but luck was in his favor when he saw the brass key lodged in it. He turned it, causing a heavy clink, then waited to see if his clatter had disturbed anyone inside.

Thirty seconds passed. A minute.

He decided it was safe. He gently pulled on the door handle but found it was jammed, probably from years of going unopened. He removed his knife from his jacket, wedged it between the cracked and jimmied the door free from its restraints. It popped open, and the air from the basement instantly engulfed his senses.

He stepped inside, feeling like he'd cracked open a museum vault. When he shone his mini-flashlight on the possessions inside, he realized it was basically as he thought. This was the room where the old man's relics came to die. It had all the makings of a typical basement: old furniture, rusty power tools, bags of cement gone hard. But between these distinct pieces were sacks of what the old man would have once called collectibles. They spilled out onto the floor in graceless heaps, and he couldn't help but bend down and inspect them. Some of them looked familiar, maybe ones he'd seen in his own collection, but he left them be. He had no care for them. There were more pressing matters to attend to.

The wooden staircase was his next point of call. Just by the sight alone he could tell they were prone to creakiness, so he stepped lightly and kept himself away from their center. At the top, he unbolted the door and found himself in a dark hallway. He hadn't seen this place in a long time, but the layout was exactly the same as he remembered. His flashlight exposed the same clock, the same wallpaper and the same gothic mirror as back in the day. It looked like old man Barry's tastes hadn't changed after all these decades.

The carpeted floor muted his journey from the hallway to the lounge, and there he saw the object of his desire, lying inertly on the couch with a remote control in his hand. What a sad sight. This is how he'd die, in front of an old black and white film that he'd probably seen a thousand times already. Even sadder was that this man probably wouldn't be missed by anyone. A cheap funeral and a small gravestone, and in the next few years, someone would say his name for the last time.

Just in time for his final breath, the end credits of the film began to roll. Old Barry lay with his mouth half-open and one arm hanging off the side of the couch. The man gripped his blade again and prepared himself. This part wasn't easy. It needed to be precise to create minimal mess. If he was off by an inch, things could go very differently than he planned, and the old man wasn't exactly in an optimal position. The couch was right up against the wall too, so he couldn't maneuver behind to get the finest angle.

He lowered his glimmering blade down to the man's fat neck, expanding and retracting in time to the symphonic music on the film score. He wanted to hear his voice again, maybe look him in the eye before he ended his life. But doing so was a risk that wasn't worth taking. Dead was more than enough.

But then, his hand suddenly spasmed, pushing the blade against the man's flesh but not with enough force to do anything. The room flashed new colors, and a resounding voice bellowed from behind him.

The film had ended and moved onto commercials, causing a sudden change in volume dynamic. Panic tempered his calm detachment until his whole core shook with dread. It all happened in a split second, and when he looked back at his would-be victim, his eyes were now wide open.

"Argh!" the old man screamed in his face, kicking his arms and legs out in a series of clumsy but effective movements. He jerked up to a sitting position and hammered on his assailant's skull with wild fists. The man cowered backward, collapsing against the wall and thrashing his blade around with reckless abandon. He felt it connect with flesh, but in the sudden change of dynamic, couldn't tell exactly where.

The old man toppled backward, hitting the couch arm and briefly losing his balance. The attacker flung towards him blade-first, sinking his weapon deep into the old man's stomach. Jets of liquid gushed from the wound, dousing them both and the yellow carpet below in warm blood. Penetrating the fleshy tissue of the stomach was a new sensation to him, much softer, like chopping up raw pig's belly. Retracting the knife brought fresh streams of blood out into the open, and the old man clutched his wound with both hands as he succumbed to the scathing pain.

His target lay on the couch again, kicking his legs in a vain attempt of protection. By now, the man's DNA must be all over this house. The revelation brought an airtight grip around the handle of his knife, which he pushed with full force into the man's throat. He felt stale breath against his face, but he didn't let go until the old man became completely motionless.

What a mess, he thought. This frail old soul had caused him more difficulty than the others combined. Had he been sloppy? Did he make mistakes? The end goal had been achieved but not the way he wanted, and that awareness induced a bout of anger that burned his temples.

He growled in rage, then release the fury in the form of a gutting stab wound to the man's heart. "Goddammit," he screamed. "You deserve this. For everything you ever did. I always hated you. I wanted you dead years ago."

He yanked out the blade like he was pulling Excalibur from the stone. He took a step back and analyzed his handiwork, not happy with any of it. He reached into his bloody jacket, grabbed what was supposed to be the jewels in the crown and held them before the old man's eyes. At least they were a perfect fit. He pushed them in until he felt the eyeballs squelch, then repositioned his eyelids to keep them in place.

Seconds later, he was back out in the night.

CHAPTER FIFTEEN

Ella lay down and in her mind's eye, saw a carousel of men's faces go round and round. First there was Jimmy Loveridge and Alan Yates, then Mark joined the ride, then Byford and Daniel Garcia. The last one, the one that seemed to switch positions each rotation, was Tobias Campbell.

She sat up and looked at the note on her nightstand, filled with some irrational fear that the note might have some ominous secrets it hadn't yet revealed. The clock told her it was six am and she'd been sitting here for hours now. That meant someone had come to her room in the middle of the night to deliver this to her.

Would there be CCTV? Could she ask the desk clerk if he saw anyone? Or would that just make the whole thing more *real?* Right now, this could be a hoax, or maybe Mark toying with her? The stress combined into a wave of burning dread that clogged her head with unneeded worries. For the past two weeks, she'd done everything she could to forget about Campbell. Since he'd sent the letter to Mia explaining their deceit, she prayed that her ordeal with him had come to an end. Maybe doing that was enough to quench his thirst for manipulation. She couldn't remember the handwriting from the other letter so she couldn't compare it, but she had a sinking feeling in her gut that he was behind this.

She looked at the facts. Tobias Campbell was in an underground prison cell, and he would never see the light of day again. He'd been awarded five life sentences, so the chances of parole were practically zero. Not to mention the fact that the courts would never release such a notorious serial killer back out into the wild. The backlash they'd get would be too severe to be worth it.

But Campbell had followers, disciples. A spider at the center of a web was how Mia described him, so he could no doubt get to her if he so desired. She'd already discovered that firsthand when he'd left a dead animal on her doorstep last month.

But why her? What did he want with her? There were billions of people he could toy with, much easier targets than her too. Was this all because she invited him into her life? Because she wanted to learn from him, so this was his twisted way of making it happen?

Ella got off the bed and went over to the nightstand table. She caught her reflection and hated the sight staring back at her: bags beneath her eyes, blotchy skin, even a stray gray hair nestled among the black. It wasn't the look of an average 29-year-old woman; it was the look of a woman in the middle of a crisis.

She scrutinized the handwriting more closely. *You didn't think I'd forgotten about you, did you?* The words were straight with no slant. The apostrophes bowed slightly to the left. The dots and crosses were penned in a straight line. There was no curvature on the *k*. The *n's* had sharp corners instead of arches. From her limited graphology knowledge, this was the handwriting of a middle-aged man. Tobias was fifty-one. It could easily be his. She had to compare it with the old letter to find out for sure.

Where had she put it? Like everything else that meant something to her, she'd put it in the gray box in her wardrobe. Maybe Jenna could retrieve it for her and send a picture.

As she grabbed her phone, another concern jumped into her head. What if this wasn't a threat at all? What if this was something else?

What if this was a request? Did Tobias want to see her in person again?

The idea chilled her nerve endings to the core. The idea of stepping in that prison again was enough to make her wretch after everything he'd put her through. Once was enough, twice was reprising the role of the fool, but three times was absolute absurdity. She wasn't going to play his games anymore, and if he was coming for her, so be it. Whether it was him, one of his minions or anyone else, she'd be ready and waiting with a chamber full of bullets for the unlucky bastard who found her.

But she had to know if this was him or not. If she had an answer, she could prepare herself for what might lie ahead. If it was a mystery, it would eat her up. She scrolled through her contacts until she found Jenna's number in her phonebook, but just as she was about to push *CALL,* a different number flashed up on the screen.

A cell number, one she didn't recognize.

"Hello?" she answered.

She knew the voice. It simply said, "There was another murder last night."

Ella pinched the root of her nose and sighed. Another layer of grief to the pile.

"I'll be right there, Sheriff," she said.

***

Ella and Byford got to the crime scene at just after seven am. The home of Barry Windham was located at 23 Hartshone Avenue, a suburban neighborhood tucked away behind a Newark Reservoir. The home in question was located on the end row but visibility from the surrounding homes was high.

"Not as discreet as the other houses," Byford said, straightening his tie as they exited the car.

"No. On first impressions, he must have targeted this house specifically."

"Agreed. Let"s see what we have."

Uniformed police officers bordered the garden to keep away onlookers. At the gate, Ella and Byford flashed their badges to the officer in charge. He waved them through.

"Hold on," he said. He clicked on his radio and pulled it to his mouth. "Feds are here."

A second later, Sheriff Hunter appeared at the front door and waved the agents up. The red ring around his eyes suggested he hadn't slept well for a while, Ella thought.

"We got a bad one," Sheriff Hunter said. "Bloodbath."

The dread began to mount. In a situation like this, the absolute best-case scenario was that the crime scene mimicked the others down to a tee. Patterns were easier to follow than chaos. If things were different, it meant the killer was evolving or experimenting, both of which made things much more difficult for investigators.

"Masks and gloves please, ladies and gentlemen." Sheriff Hunter handed them the hardware. They put them on and walked into the home, first entering onto a carpeted hallway. The smell of coppery blood took center stage, overwhelming the faint aroma of mahogany Ella picked up from the furniture. Even with his mask on, Byford covered his nose.

When they turned the corner into the lounge, the true horror made itself known. This time, the coins were yet to be removed from the victim's eye sockets, so Ella was able to see this monstrosity in the flesh.

"Christ," she said, averting her eyes for a moment. "This is atrocious. This poor man." The victim must have been in his sixties or older, on the slightly larger side too. He lay sprawled on the couch, two

83

glimmering coins concealing his eyes, three wounds decorating his body. She turned to Byford, who was consuming the scene with a look of unease.

"You okay, Nigel?"

"Yeah," he said. "It's just unbelievable. The things we can do. This doesn't even look like something from this world."

Ella was a little surprised at his display of emotion. Maybe he was human after all. "What do we know so far?" She directed her question to the sheriff.

"This is Barry Windham, 62 years old, lives alone. He worked as an electrician until last year."

Banker, antique dealer, electrician. When it came to the world of coins, one of those things was not like the others.

"Who called it in?" asked Byford.

"The next door neighbor. She heard a scream around one am, then she heard some banging. That's when she called us. We got here pretty quickly but didn't catch sight of anyone. We patrolled the area all night too. Nothing."

"A disturbance. That didn't happen with the others," Ella said. Up by the sofa, a technician knelt down and took some close-up photos of Barry's wounds. When she left, she signaled to the agents that the scene was theirs.

Ella moved closer to the body and started at the familiar part – the neck. All of the victims, including this one, had deep lacerations to the neck. But here, something was different. The other cuts had been precise, intended, almost surgically accurate. But the deep cut across Barry Windham's neck was anything but. Fragments of bone and muscle tissue were visible, and if death was the goal, there was no need for this to be the case. In contrast to the precision shown with the other victims, Barry Windham's death blow was chaotic and uncontrolled.

"A lot more stabbing went on," Sheriff Hunter said.

Ella continued down the body, coming to the next wound near the heart. Not quite through the heart, maybe an inch away. She suddenly remembered what Daniel Garcia had said about Santerian sacrifices and panicked a little, wondering for a second if she hadn't made another grave mistake. She looked at the coins in the eyes, finding these ones were both facing tails.

She took a moment to consider it. These were the facts. She couldn't change them, but the other victims didn't follow suit. If Ripley was here, she would tell Ella exactly that. *Mold the theories to fit the facts, not the other way around.* With that in mind, she erased the word Santeria from her head and focused on the dead body in front of her.

Next in line was a puncture to the victim's stomach. About two inches wide, meaning the blade had penetrated the flesh and then been dragged down. This wasn't an indication of a planned attack. Again, it was untidy, almost desperate.

"These two got into a fight, but our unsub managed to subdue him."

"This blood spatter runs from the couch to the wall," Byford added. "At some point, they battled over here, then our killer moved him back to the couch."

"I think so. We know our killer strikes people when they're sleeping, so maybe Barry managed to catch him before the killer attacked."

"Either that or he cut him off at the pass." Byford inspected the blood stains against the wall. "The spatter is lighter here, so he most likely stabbed him here first. Either they got into an altercation, or Barry was waiting for him when he turned this corner."

Ella eyed the victim from top to bottom again. "No, look. This blanket is wrapped around Barry"s ankle. That suggests he jumped up from this spot in a hurry."

Byford came over and inspected the victim. "True. Good observation."

Ella had seen all of the wounds she needed to. There was only one other thing left to check. "Sheriff, can you call a forensics agent back?"

"Sure," he disappeared around the corner, returning a few seconds later with the same forensics technician who'd taken the pictures. Sheriff Hunter pointed at Ella and the technician came over.

"Some questions?" the woman asked. Ella could see behind her mask she was of Asian descent but couldn't tell anymore.

"Would it be possible to remove these coins? We'd like to check something."

The technician nodded then knelt down in front of the couch. With her gloved hands, she enlarged the area around the eye with one hand and removed the coin with the other. She placed it inside a small plastic bag and passed it to Ella. Byford and Hunter both glanced closely at it too.

It was a gold coin this time, with Asian characters around the edges and a swirling dragon on the face. On the other side, a bald man's face. This time, there were no English markings whatsoever.

"What's that, Japanese again?" Hunter asked.

"No, I don't recognize these symbols at all. This isn't Kanji. It might be Korean or…"

"It's Chinese," the technician said. "That's President Kai-shek on the face."

"Oh, thank you," Ella said. "Can you read these symbols?" She passed the coin to her.

"I can indeed." The technician took it and held the bag to her eye-level. "*Hope and prosperity under Kai-shek's rule. Shen-Si Province. 1964.*"

The atmosphere changed when the date hit the air. The rush came surging back and Ella had to stop herself from clenching her fist in elation. "What was that year? 1964?" she asked.

"Yeah," the technician pointed to a small inscription at the bottom edge of the coin. "It's written a little different on coins to save space. Usually, it would be seven characters long, but they've just used the individual numerals here, so it's only four. Does that help?"

Ella didn't need any more confirmation. The coins at every crime scene were from 1964. It couldn't be a coincidence. "Yes. Thank you so much."

The technician checked the second coin on the body. "This one's the same. Exactly the same coin. Is there anything else you need?"

"No." Ella glanced between Byford and Sheriff. "You guys?"

They both shook their heads.

"Feel free to take them for testing," Ella said. She stood up and headed away from the scene, coming to a conservatory door leading out into the garden. The glass panel reached from floor to ceiling. If this unsub came in through the rear, he'd have been able to see his target sleeping.

"Sheriff, do we know how the perp got inside?" she asked. Sheriff Hunter joined her at the window.

"Nope. That's something you might be able to help with. When we got here, every door was locked."

"Every door. We had to use the enforcer on the front to get in, and even that was bolted from the inside."

From what Ella gleaned from cop talk over the years, the enforcer was a battering ram. "So he locked the doors on the way out."

"Could be," the sheriff said. "He could have lifted a key."

"He could have, but why? He didn't at the other scenes, he just left the doors open. And it's not like this is a murder of convenience. Our unsub *wants* people to find these dead bodies."

The sheriff took his mask off and threw it on a side table. "Prolong the process, maybe. I dunno. You're the behavioral expert."

Yes, she was, and she had to find out how this unsub gained access. She went back out the front of the house and looked at it with a criminal eye. Locked front door, no breach-able windows. The only other possible route was through the garden. She moved to the outside gate, a relatively low iron gate that could be easily bested. She unhooked the latch and made her way round the side of the house. There, she found herself on the other side of the large glass pane. Locked again, and the windows here didn't open anywhere near enough for a grown man to fit through.

Ella took a few steps back, surveyed the building, and entertained the idea that this unsub might have climbed up the drainpipe to an upstairs window. Her eyes followed the pipe along the foundations of the roof, watching it snake round to the left and then miraculously disappear.

"Huh?" she said aloud. She moved around to the left, and there, sitting in a very narrow gap between the house and the fence was a set of steps. Ella approached them and found they descended down to the bottom level.

She followed them down, moving a trash can out of the way and coming to a large red door. It wasn't quite sitting flush in its frame. Someone had recently opened it, she realized

One tug of the handle opened the contents within. Ella moved into a small basement, tripping over a pile of power tools upon arrival. The morning light illuminated it all, and it wasn't the discarded chairs or the old motor engine that drew her attention first; it was the sacks.

"Oh my God," she said, and suddenly, this case looked a lot different than it did before. "Byford, Hunter. Get down here," she shouted. "You're going to want to see this."

She had everything she needed. This was it. This was how she was going to catch him.

CHAPTER SIXTEEN

Ella rushed back to the precinct with a head full of ghosts, vague ideas with the potential to fully manifest with enough energy. What she'd found in the basement had completely changed her course. Up until now, the jigsaw pieces had all been scattered to the wind, but this morning she uncovered the force that pulled them together.

They'd found coins. Thousands upon thousands of them. Barry Windham must have been a coin collector once upon a time but had since given up the hobby for whatever reason. Could this killer be targeting people in the coin collector trade? If so, how did the first two victims fit into it? That's what she was going to find out.

In her office, she loaded up her desk with paperwork. For this, she needed physical copies, not words on a screen. Holding something in her hand helped make everything more authentic. Byford followed in after her.

"So, nothing to do with religion or sacrifice," he said with a note of pretension. Ella was happy to admit when she was wrong, a trait a lot of people needed to adopt in her profession, she thought.

"Nothing at all. I went down a wrong path and I'm sorry."

"I could have told you that yesterday. Oh well," he said.

Ella wasn't about to get into another argument with the man. Sometimes, he seemed like he had the potential to be a great partner. Other times, he made a great advertisement for working solo.

"You did, and I'm sorry I didn't listen. But we've got a ton of evidence that backs this theory up, so how about we dive in and crack it open?"

Byford rested his hands on the table. "I'm with you on this one. The coin link is clear with this victim. Not so much with the others, but maybe that's because we haven't looked hard enough. And this 1964 link could be what helps us find this culprit."

The 1964 link was undeniable, but Ella still didn't know what it symbolized. These men were all different ages, so it wasn't their birth years. It couldn't be the unsub's year of birth either, since that would make him almost 60 years old. A 60-year-old, no matter how healthy or athletic, couldn't pull off the necessary guile to carry out these attacks. It was rare, almost unheard of, for a serial killer to begin their killing career so late in life.

She thought of the first two victims, a former bank manager and antiques dealer. How could she dig into their lives? If they had a link to the world of coin collecting, she needed to find it. The first victim, Alan Yates, began as a bank manager and then retired in his fifties to focus on charity work. She sifted through her papers looking for everything she had on Alan Yates, scanned it, and found no link to the coin world. Opposite her, Byford buried his head in the new reports.

Ella sat down and pulled her laptop closer. She had to go virtual to find something on him. She searched online for *ALAN YATES NEWARK DELAWARE* and came up with over 3 million results, way too many to sift through. She added the word philanthropy and narrowed it down significantly. She began scrolling through the results.

"Wow, looks like Alan Yates was quite the donor." She found mentions of schools, hospitals, and charities on the first page of results alone. *LOCAL BENEFACTOR GIFTS PPE TO HOSPITAL* was the result she first dug into. The article had a picture of Alan Yates, shaking the hand of a woman in nurse scrubs. She scanned for anything useful in the article but found nothing.

She continued on down the page. The next result detailed Alan's donation to a local charity for underprivileged children. Books, toys, games, clothes, electronics. The guy was a real hero, Ella thought. The fact such a generous man could be taken so cruelly filled her with a dreadful awareness of her own mortality.

"Found anything?" Byford asked.

"Alan Yates gave away a small fortune but I'm not finding a link to the coin collecting world."

"Maybe try collector pages or see if there are communities in the area."

Ella didn't think it would be much use. "If Alan was a collector, we'd have found coins in his house. The sheriff said he searched that place high and low and found nothing. Same with Jimmy Loveridge."

"I guess," Byford shrugged, offering nothing more. Ella wished he'd be a little more enthusiastic at times.

She scoured five more articles, finding more of the same. Alan seemed to make notable donations on a regular basis, like he was eager to give away his entire fortune. As a last resort, she flipped to the images section and mostly found the pictures she'd already seen in the articles. She scrolled through. Alan smiling in a group of children, Alan shaking hands with the mayor, Alan at an awards ceremony.

The images decreased in quality as she reached the bottom of the page. By now, she was finding things completely unrelated to the task at hand. She fell back in the chair and let the white glow of the screen engulf her vision, then she fell into a daydream as thoughts of the strange note back in her motel room returned. The recent discovery of Barry Windham's collecting habit had made her all but forget about the note, but when the chaos died down, Tobias Campbell was still there haunting her reflections. He was two thousand miles away, but right next to her at the same time.

For a fleeting moment, she wondered if the best possible solution to all this was to visit Maine Correctional one last time, sneak in a Glock .22 and put a bullet in his Campbell's heart. The fantasy quickly became all-consuming, and it wasn't until a minute later that she realized she was staring at a very familiar image on her computer screen.

Ella gripped the table edge and shook away any thoughts of Tobias. When she was back in the present, she became aware of the fact that the last image on her search results featured that of a small child, glowing blonde hair, beaming smile like he'd just drank an ocean of chocolate milk. The image quality was low, like it had been pulled from a decades-old news piece, and the child in question bore no resemblance to any child she'd seen in her lifetime.

But what caught her attention was the object in his hand.

"Nigel," she said. "Here."

Byford rushed up from his chair and joined her on the other side of the table. Ella enlarged the image, finding it was barely three-hundred by three-hundred pixels.

"Oh, lord. That's…," he squinted his eyes. "The Japanese yen coin. The one they found at the Yates scene."

Ella's first thought that this was some massive accident on her part and that she'd altered her search results during her mind-drift. She checked everything again. No, she hadn't. The results still said *ALAN YATES NEWARK PHILANTHROPY.* She clicked into the corresponding article and the page loaded a completely white slate.

"It's a dead link," Byford said.

Ella slammed her palm against the table. "Shit. There's gotta be a way in."

She copied the link location, pasted it in the URL bar and got the same blank page. She tried a different browser with the same result.

"Give it up, it's not going to work."

Ella remembered Mia saying something about technology the last time the Internet let them down. She couldn't remember the exact line, but it was something like *stop demanding so much from technology and start demanding it from yourself.* Ella interpreted it to mean that if you wanted results, technological or not, you had to apply yourself.

"The page must be cached somewhere," she said. On the blank white page, she dug into the HTML code through the browser's command console. Her heart began to pound when she saw five text files, two image files and a bunch of extensions she didn't recognize. There was something here.

She extracted the first text file to a Notepad document and found it was the first paragraph of the dead article. "Yes!" she called. "We got it."

19th March, 2002. A local investment banker and benefactor put smiles on a lot of faces this week after showing up unannounced to a local school armed with sacks full of goodies for the children to enjoy. Alan Yates surprised the schoolchildren at Wood Green's School For Disadvantaged Children with cases of toys, board games, creative tools, and Nintendo devices.

"I'm not seeing anything about coins," Byford said. Ella wished he'd be a little more patient. Ella extracted the next paragraph.

But one particular stack of items from Mr. Yates's stash was the biggest hit among the children: his bags of old coins. "Sometimes we get the odd foreign coin in the stashes at the bank." Mr. Yates went on to say. "We don't have much use for them, so I take them out and save them. I know Pogs are all the rage these days, so I thought the kids would have more use for them than me!"

"Got you!" Ella said. She clenched her fists and hammered them on the table in exhilaration. "I knew it! Alan used to gift coins to kids. That's gotta be part of this whole thing."

Byford took a step back, rubbed his chin forcefully. "It's interesting to say the least, but how?"

Ella realized now that Byford was one of those people who was quick to offer problems but rarely solutions. "I don't know, but it's a starting point. Now, if we can establish that Jimmy Loveridge had some link to this world, we've got a solid connection we can explore."

"This article is from twenty years ago, though."

Ella didn't reply, and instead waited for Byford to offer something other than a setback. He offered nothing, so she took it upon herself.

91

"Didn't Jimmy's wife say something about pawn shops? That Jimmy dealt with them?"

"She did."

"Let's go and have a word with the one she mentioned. They might be able to tell us something."

"Alright, let me just finish up," Byford said.

She read the rest of the article while she waited for her partner, finding nothing of value. Alan Yates used to find foreign coins in his shipments, so gave them away to children to play with. She remembered Pogs from back when she was a kid, and Alan was right, the kids would have loved them. Pretty creative judgment on Alan's part, she thought.

To finish, she checked the two image files. The first was the picture of the smiling boy with the coin, the second was an image she hadn't yet seen, and one made her skin break out in goosebumps.

"Oh my God," she said. She thought the cocktail of exhaustion and stress was forcing her eyes to play tricks on her. "Nigel, look at this."

"What now?" he asked as he got to his seat. He grabbed his jacket before he sauntered over. When he got to the screen, he too froze in shock. "Holy f...."

The picture showed Alan Yates as a younger man, smiling ear to ear while holding two coins over his eyes.

CHAPTER SEVENTEEN

Ella parked their vehicle around 200 feet away from their destination. One of the advantages of being in law enforcement was the parking flexibility but finding spaces in a busy city like Newark was still an arduous task. Ella found an empty curb outside a hardware store where she wouldn't obstruct traffic.

Aces & Eights was an old brick-and-mortar shop on Dragon Run Road in downtown Delaware. It had a pinstripe canopy cascading down from the roof, immaculately clean and surprisingly appealing, Ella thought. The shop window announced *WE BUY GOLD* in giant letters that were impossible to ignore. Ella suddenly realized that she'd never actually been in a pawn shop in her life.

Tolling wind chimes announced their entrance through the wooden door. The interior smelled of fresh pine and lemon, and it seemed there wasn't an inch of space that didn't boast some ancient relic. The path through the shop was determined by a small strip that could barely stand two people. It ran through the store linearly, like some kind of manual amusement ride. To Ella's left she saw two elongated masks staring back at her, looking like they belonged to some faraway African tribe. All the bizarre stuff seemed to be at the front, while the rear was decked with bikes, guitars, electronics and jewelry.

They moved to the counter and found it deserted. Ella shouted for assistance.

"Hello. Anyone here?"

"Be right out," a voice replied. Seconds later, a gentleman appeared from a back room, sweating. "Sorry, some heavy stuff back there. Are you guys okay?"

The gentleman was as stocky as they came. Gray hair decorated his face, from his windswept hair to his gigantic beard that reached his chest. If Ella had to guess, he was about fifty years old. He wore a gray vest that revealed his tree trunk-like arms. Not muscular as such but looked like they could hold a few pounds.

"We don't mean to bother you, sir, but I'm Agent Dark and this is Agent Byford with the FBI. We're looking for the owner of this store."

"That'll be me. I'm Ace. FBI, you say? Well, I didn't do it, I promise," he laughed.

"We're sure you didn't. We're actually investigating a homicide case and we believe you may have known the victim."

"Old Jimmy," Ace chimed in before Ella could finish. "Yeah, I heard. I had a feeling the cops would come knocking actually. I don't know all the details but it's shocking. Appalling."

"You expected us, sir?" Byford asked.

"Yeah. And less of the *sir*. Call me Ace. I named this shop because my eight kids help me run it."

Ella put the dots together. "Wow, eight children? Do you sell TVs in here? Because I think you need one for your bedroom."

"Zing!" Jimmy laughed. "They've all grown up and left me now. I'd have another eight if my wife was still around. But anyway, me and Jimmy were as close as any married couple, so ask me anything. I got all day."

Ella appreciated Ace's cooperation. A lot of people would be afraid of being so helpful in case it cast them in a suspicious light. Given Ace's size, she doubted he could sneak into three homes unobserved.

"Thank you. Jimmy's wife said you and he sometimes had spats. Can you tell us about that?"

"Spats?" Ace laughed. "She's talking out of her backside. This is a man's business, and banter comes with the territory. Me and Jimmy might have disagreed on a few things but nine times out of ten, we were like brothers. I had a lot of respect for the old man."

Ella decided to rummage around their relationship before getting to the real question. "What did you disagree on?"

"Prices mostly. His store is a cat's hair away from mine. Ain't no one gonna buy a vase from him when I've got the same thing for half the price. He was always telling me to put my prices up, but I told him there was no point. If I did that, neither of us would get the sale."

"Sounds like classic competitor pricing," Byford said.

Ace pulled his beard and twisted it around. Ella had to wonder how that thing didn't itch his face off. "Totally. But he had his antiques lovers; I have my bargain hounds. We both got our own niche, but we overlapped when it came to stuff like ornaments, jewelry, coins. Everyday stuff."

Ella and Byford caught each other's stare when Ace mentioned the magic word.

"You touched on something we're very interested in there, Ace. Do you know if Jimmy had any involvement with coins at all? Specifically rare coins?"

Ace rested his hands on the countertop. "Coins you say? Well, you won't find an antique dealer that *doesn't* sell coins, but yeah, Jimmy sold a few."

Ella felt the walls of this getting smaller. Whenever she got a connection like this, it sent her numb for a few seconds, then the dopamine high kicked in. It was the rush she lived for.

"He did? Do you know what type of coins? Or whether he had any regular buyers?"

"Umm, well I'm not sure about Jimmy's particular transactions or anything. I know he sometimes sold coins by the bundle. Can I ask why coins are so special here?"

"It's confidential," Byford jumped in, abrupt as ever.

Ella thought that maybe they should give a little back. Ace and Jimmy were clearly close, and it didn't seem fair to not clue him in on some aspects of his friend's murder.

"We can't say too much, but two coins were found on Jimmy's body. We believe they may have some significance to the crime, like perhaps a wronged client looking for vengeance. We still don't know all the answers yet."

Ace retreated a little in light of the new information. He was probably picturing the scene in his head. People had a tendency to keep a vicarious distance from the realities of murder, but when presented with specific details, it made it all the more real.

"Christ almighty. I'm sorry to hear that. But now that you mention it, I might have something you can use." Ace disappeared back into his stock room. Ella heard him fumble around, then he returned with a wooden board. He spun it around to show the agents. It had around ten mugshots pinned to it.

"What's this?" Byford asked.

"See this? These are all the guys banned from my shop. Rude people, thieves, general assholes. You name it."

Ella skimmed the photos and didn't recognize anyone. Some of the photos were close-up portraits while others were blurry CCTV-screened snaps. "Looks like a friendly bunch," she said.

Ace pulled off the picture second from the right. "See this guy? This is Aleister Black. A scummy piece of work to say the least." He passed the picture to Ella. The man in the photograph had both sides of his head shaved, with long black hair stemming from the top. He had piercing blue eyes, thin features and a scar through his lip. On the shaved parts of his head were tribal tattoos.

"What did he do?" Ella asked.

"To me personally? Not a whole lot. He's been in my shop a few times, but he just looks around and leaves. Gives me a real creepy vibe, to be honest."

"Is that all?" asked Byford.

"No. This guy is a collector. An obsessive one. I think he's got some mental issues because he acts all weird like. No eye contact, twitches, you know the sort."

It seemed a vast generalization, but Ella didn't want to mention it. The chances of their unsub having some kind of behavioral issues was almost certain, so this Aleister Black gentleman was definitely worth checking out.

"Do you know what he collects?"

"Coins," Ace said. He let the silence punctuate his statement. Ella's head jerked in the direction of her partner. Byford looked as surprised as she did.

"Really? He's a coin collector. He doesn't look the type."

"Like I said, he's got problems. But there's a coin dealer down in New Castle; apparently Aleister beat the heck out of him for not parting with one of his treasures. Jimmy had some run-ins with Aleister too as far as I know. It was Jimmy who got me this picture, actually."

That was all Ella needed to hear. They needed to check this man out. If he'd committed assault, chances were that he was in the police database. The picture of him looked like an official mugshot photo, too.

"Thanks so much, Ace," Ella said. "This is fantastic."

"You're welcome. When you catch this scumbag, give him one from me, yeah?" Ace balled up his fist and punched the air.

"We will. One last thing before we go," said Ella. "Could you give us a list of any regular clients who buy coins from here? Ideally ones who've made recent purchases."

"I only sold to one guy and the old bastard died weeks ago. Heart attack, I think. I'll dig through my records for you though, just in case I've missed anyone. If you need me, I actually live upstairs here, so don't be a stranger. Adios."

The agents left the pawn shop and went back to the car. Ella started up and headed back to the precinct. In her pocket, she felt her phone buzz, and decided that today was the day her relationship changed for the better. The only man she had time for today was a violent, obsessive coin collector.

***

Before she tracked this man down, she needed to know everything about him. In her office, Ella found Aleister Black's police file and went through it with surgical precision.

"Ace was right, this Aleister guy attacked a man in New Castle last year," she said to Byford beside her.

"Did he go to prison?"

Ella continued on. "No, just community service. But it doesn't stop there. He's been arrested three times in the past five years. Violence, disorderly behavior. Murder is a natural progression from that."

"Not a bad find," said Byford. "What's his employment record? Surely someone this unstable must be a drifter."

Ella checked the next section. "No, actually. Looks like he worked for Quanta Services Newark."

Byford scratched the side of his head. "Quanta? Where've I heard that name recently?"

Ella moved her fingers off her keyboard. "Have you? I've never heard of them. Who are they?"

"They're an electrical company. Branches all over the country." Byford went over to his pile of paperwork and rustled through. He picked up the police report from Barry Windham's murder and leafed through. "Here, look."

Ella took the file and felt her heart skip when she saw the words. "Holy crap. Barry Windham worked for them too."

Byford snapped his fingers. "Bingo. We've got a link. I'm liking the sound of this suspect."

Ella felt the same. Just from his picture alone, she could picture this man breaking into homes, slashing throats, and leaving behind bizarre relics. It felt like the pieces fit perfectly well.

"So we know he has links to Jimmy Loveridge and Barry Windham. I'm going to see if I can find any link to the first victim and then we need to pay this man a visit." She thought about Alan Yates. He'd been retired for ten years but worked for JPMorgan Chase before he settled down. She devoured all of the text on the page, finding no mention of banks whatsoever. There was no more text to consume.

"Hang on," Byford said. "Didn't it say Aleister vandalized some buildings in town?"

Ella scrolled back, quickly catching Byford's train of thought. "Yes, it did. Good thinking. Let me check." Her excitement was short-lived.

"No. He vandalized a pharmacy and a grocery store. Damn it." She skimmed through the file again to see if she'd missed anything, focusing on the stand-out terms."

"It doesn't matter, it's enough. Let's get his address and…"

"Hold on a second," Ella interrupted, landing on a word that caught her attention. "Alan Yates. The sheriff brought us the coins from all of the crime scenes, remember?"

"Yeah. What about them?"

"Do you remember what kind of coins they were?"

Byford browsed his file again. "Japanese coins. One thousand yen. Okinawa 1964 according to this file."

There it was. Another spark. More pieces falling into place. "Look. Aleister Black lived abroad for a year. Look at the location."

Byford leaned down to see the screen more clearly. "Well damn. Okinawa, Japan."

"Come on," Ella said, pushing herself up in haste. "I've got his address. Time to meet this man for ourselves."

CHAPTER EIGHTEEN

The address listed in the police file was a gentrified apartment building called Apollo House, perhaps at one time a warehouse or industrial building. The front had recently been stuccoed, and all four apartments in the front had leaded-glass bay windows.

Ella circled past the building and parked just out of sight. She knew the mindset of a killer, and if Aleister Black was one, he wasn't going to answer the door to two strangers. She got out of the car, checked the mailboxes, and found that number 1 belonged to an A.B. Behind the window blinds, she saw a silhouette moving back and forth.

As it wasn't yet nine am, Ella devised a plan. She got back in the car and told Byford to wait with her. Approaching suspects in a public area made them less likely to turn hostile. It was one of Mia's techniques. In their own homes, suspects maintained an air of supremacy. On neutral ground, it was a different story.

They watched the pedestrian traffic up and down the road. After ten minutes or so, Ella got restless. She got out of the car, crossed the street, leaned against a telephone pole took out her phone. She pretended to have a conversation. Cell phones were, hands down, the best surveillance prop ever invented, she thought.

Finally, the door to the apartment complex opened. The first person to walk out of the building was an older woman, well-dressed and accessorized to the nines. When she reached the sidewalk she stopped, rummaged through her purse then stormed back inside the building. She'd obviously forgotten something. A minute later, a second resident emerged. A much different picture this time.

He was dressed in a black overcoat, tight jeans, and heavy black boots. His dark hair had been tied back, exposing the swirly tribal tattoos on the side of his head. From what Ella could tell, one of them was in the shape of a dragon. His skin was alarmingly pale, like he hadn't seen the sun in decades.

The man moved across the street, keeping his gaze to the ground. When he reached the car, Ella called out to him.

"Excuse me, Mr. Black?"

Aleister looked up from the ground and locked eyes with his caller. They darted around, finally landing on Ella's knees. Ella recognized it as a sign of timidity or more severe mental health issues.

"Do I know you?" he asked. His posture betrayed neither aggression nor escape. Instead, he looked pleasantly curious, if a little afraid.

Within a few seconds of their meeting, she saw the symptoms Ace mentioned. Aleister seemed unsteady on his feet, his limbs twitching in no particular pattern.

"You don't. My name's Agent Dark and I'm with the FBI. Could we talk for a moment?"

Aleister looked at her badge, then back down to Ella's lower half. In the spring morning light, his eyes were a pale blue, almost colorless. A harsh contrast to his entirely black profile.

"FBI? Okay, but I can't imagine what I could tell you. Or your partner over there."

Ella laughed. She hadn't expected this man to be so observant. Or maybe she and Byford had just been careless. "Well spotted. Do you know why we're here?"

Aleister folded his arms and shifted his weight onto one leg. Ella didn't quite know what to make of this man. Violent offender? Troubled autist? Something else?

"Yes. It's because of the killings, isn't it?"

Another unexpected comment, but not a desired one. "It is. You know about them?"

"Yeah. I know all about them. I read the news. A lot." Aleister began to shift his weight across his body and back again, like he was dancing to some invisible beat. Ella was struggling to get a feel of this man's personality, but his criminal history spoke for itself. He'd attacked a man, vandalized buildings, and engaged in disorderly conduct. Even if he was struggling mentally, they couldn't be overlooked.

"Were you familiar with the victims?" Ella asked, already knowing the answer but wanting to gauge his honesty levels.

"I knew Jimmy, but everyone knew Jimmy. That's all."

Ella picked up on his language. Referring to a recently deceased victim in the past tense, especially when it was someone you had a connection with, was considered a red flag. Not definitive proof by any means, but worth taking into consideration. Ella saw Byford had exited the car and was standing beside it now.

"You had a run-in with him, correct?"

Aleister dug his hands into his coat pockets and began to sway. His shoulders twitched as he spoke.

"Once. But I went back and said sorry. I made a mistake."

"Can you tell me what happened?" Ella asked. She double-checked her pistol and handcuffs were within grabbing distance. Something told her that this man had an aggressive side to him, and it was only a matter of time before it rose to the surface.

"I asked Jimmy to keep an item for me. He said he would, but when I went to buy it, he'd sold it to someone else. The other buyer offered him more money. It broke my heart. I really wanted the item."

Aleister's language appeared very clinical, almost rehearsed. Ella wasn't sure if this was how he always behaved or whether it was an act. The psychopath's mask only slipped when they were backed into a corner.

"What was it, this item?" she asked.

"A coin. A really great one. I collect them. This one would have completed my 1942 Soviet collection."

"Mr. Black, are you aware that rare coins were discovered at each crime scene? Given your previous encounter with Jimmy Loveridge, you can see why we have a need to question you," Ella said.

Byford slowly walked over to the scene and stood behind the suspect. Aleister sensed him, turned around, then began retreating back towards the apartment building.

"Don't go anywhere," Byford said. "Stay right there."

Aleister froze in place then held up his palms to the agents. "Please, I don't like being surrounded. Can you back away a few steps please?"

"I'm sorry, sir, but you're wanted in regard to a murder investigation. We can't take this lightly. Please can you come with us?"

Dammit, Byford, Ella thought. *I had this under control.* She wished he'd read the room a little bit before jumping right in with protocol. Sometimes, protocol wasn't all it was cracked up to be

"No," Aleister said as he backtracked further. "I'm not going with you. You can't make me."

"Please, Aleister, let's relax a little here. We're not…"

"Get away from me, both of you." His twitches became more intense, losing balance as he tried to out-maneuver the agents. Suddenly, Aleister tripped and stumbled into Ella. She grabbed him to hold him upright, but Aleister pushed her hard against the streetlamp. Her spine cracked against it, taking the wind out of her, and seeing what he'd done, the suspect took flight.

His intended direction was across the road, but Byford was immediately on the man. He shoulder-tackled Aleister to the ground with a sickening crack, all while Aleister desperately clawed at his attacker. Ella worked through the pain, running over to the theater of conflict to help her partner. Aleister wormed his way out of Byford's grip, but Ella was waiting for him. She took him by the wrist, twisted it behind his back and extended the shoulder to the point of discomfort. For some reason, maybe a deep-rooted sympathy, she didn't want to hurt this man.

"Aleister, we need to take you into custody, okay?"

"No. Please don't. I haven't done anything wrong," he cried. "Please don't handcuff me. I don't like being restrained."

"I won't, if you promise to come with us, okay?" She relieved the pressure, keeping him pressed against the floor with her knee. "We're not arresting you. We just need to talk."

Aleister pushed his forehead against the cold ground. "Okay. I will."

But as Ella took a step back, Byford jumped in place. Before she could protest, he'd locked handcuffs on the suspect's wrists. Aleister's response was a full-blown breakdown, lashing his feet out and screaming deafening cries.

"Nigel, why?" Ella asked. "You didn't need to do that."

Byford pulled the suspect up, doing nothing to quench his outburst. Ella looked around and saw all of the residents standing outside the apartment building, watching in awe.

"He's a murder suspect. I'm not naïve enough to trust him." Byford hauled the man into the back of their car and locked him in. Aleister's screaming stopped, but through the glass, Ella saw him hyperventilating.

She didn't have a good feeling about this. Something was going on, but something was very strange about it. Back at the precinct, they needed to have a long talk with Aleister Black.

CHAPTER NINETEEN

Watching him through the two-way mirror of the interrogation room, Aleister Black reminded Ella of a child. His mannerisms, his outbursts, his inability to regulate his emotions. But even so, did that mean he was innocent? A mentally stunted individual is still capable of committing atrocities, and besides, there was no guarantee this wasn't all just an Oscar-worthy performance.

Sheriff Hunter approached Ella, stale smoke lingering on his clothes. "Do you think this is our guy?"

Ella didn't quite know how to respond. If she had to make a guess, the scales tipped in favor of guilty, but there was enough reasonable doubt to second-guess her assumption. "It's a coin flip," she said. She suddenly gasped at her error. "Sorry. I didn't mean that."

"Easy mistake to make, given the circumstances. What do you have on this fella?"

"What don't we have? He's a coin collector. He has a history of criminal activity. He got into a fight with Jimmy Loveridge. He works for the same company Barry Windham did. He even spent time in Japan, the same part where the coins at a crime scene came from."

Sheriff Hunter's mouth fell open. "Well, shit. I think any judge in the world would put that guy behind bars in a second."

"It doesn't look good for him, I'll admit. It's just..."

"What? You don't think it's him?"

"Cops always told me about that gut feeling they had. Like, they can just look at a suspect and *know* they're either guilty or innocent."

"Oh yeah. I know that. It's a real double-edger."

"Yeah, well I always thought that was just bullcrap. But now I'm in this job, I get the same feeling."

"It's called intuition," Hunter said. "We pick up on things outside of the usual; our brains just don't understand it."

A simplified version, Ella thought, but pretty accurate. "Yeah. There's something about him that I just don't get. He's impossible to read. I have my doubts, I'll be honest."

Byford joined them with a coffee in hand. He hadn't gotten Ella one and she was getting desperate for a caffeine hit by now. She'd hadn't had one today and the withdrawal symptoms were starting to show.

"Shall we?" he asked.

The coffee would have to wait. "Okay. Let's present him with the evidence."

"No, let's accuse him of being the murderer," Byford said. "We might as well start as we mean to go on."

Byford was showing his time served, Ella thought. Immediate accusations were the old school approach to FBI interrogations, but that method had long been replaced by a more natural, conversational approach.

"The accusation style died out years ago," Ella said. "It's not a viable interrogation style anymore."

"Yes, it is. It's advised in situations with ample evidence, which we have."

"We don't have ample evidence. We have a few tangible links. Nothing solid connects Aleister Black to these crime scenes."

Byford conceded. "Alright, let's do it your way. Come on."

Ella couldn't believe her partner wanted to use that technique. It had been considered outdated during her entire time at the FBI. Maybe Byford needed a refresher course. With a little tension between them, the two agents entered the room to a cowering suspect. Aleister Black's arms folded right around his body, like a child clutching an invisible teddy. The two agents took a seat opposite him.

"Mr. Black, we're sorry for bringing you in like this, but you understand why, don't you?" said Ella.

Aleister nodded. His head jerked to the left. A new twitch Ella hadn't seen yet. This anxiety must have been hell for him.

"Can you tell us about your fight with Mr. Loveridge? What happened exactly?"

"I just screamed at him. I didn't hit him. I apologized the next day."

"Right. And what about your attack on the dealer in New Castle? It says in your record that you assaulted him."

"That was the man who bought the coin off Jimmy. I just punched him in the nose, but I didn't do any damage. A guy like me doesn't punch so good."

Ella did notice the distinct lack of muscle tone in the man. Combined with the color of his skin, malnutrition was a safe bet.

"Okay, and your file says you lived in Okinawa, Japan, for a while? Can you tell us about that?"

Aleister smiled for the first time since they met. Maybe he had some good memories of his time there, memories that he remembered through his coin collection, perhaps.

"Yes, I did. I wanted to get away. People in this country aren't so nice to people like me. But in Japan, no one batted an eyelid to me. I felt like I belonged there, so I stayed as long as I could. But you need a Visa to live there, and I didn't have one. After nine months, I had to come back."

"Did you happen to bring any coins back for your collection?" asked Byford.

"Yes. Lots. Rare ones too. Japan has lots of great coins."

Ella saw in Byford's expression that he saw this as a *gotcha* moment, but Ella didn't feel the same way. A guilty man, regardless of their naivety, wouldn't mention such a thing.

"Mr. Black, a rare Japanese coin was found at the home of one of our victims. What do you have to say about that?"

Aleister looked up from the table for the first time since he entered the room. "What type of coin was it?"

"One thousand yen. Okinawa 1964. Mean anything to you?"

"It means a lot, but it's not rare. You can find those things very easily."

"Do you have any in your collection?" asked Byford.

"Several. Every collector does."

Again, with the admission. Ella was really struggling to see the light here. "Mr. Black, what do you do for work?" she asked.

"Warehouse."

"You work for an electrical company, is that right?"

"Yes. Quanta. Why?"

"How long have you been there?" Ella asked.

"In total, ten years. I worked there for seven years, then I left to go to Japan. Then I started working there when I came home."

"So, you must be pretty familiar with some of the other employees there," said Byford, catching on to Ella's thought process.

"I know everybody. It's a big place, but I know all the names and faces. Part of my Asperger's. I can't forget something once I've committed it to memory."

Ella knew all about that. Lots of things she wished she'd forget, she couldn't. Not even tragic things, just minor things like a random stranger's birth date. "You have a photographic memory?" she asked. She'd never met anyone else with one before.

105

"Not exactly. I just have a compulsion to commit every detail I come across to memory. I see my brain as a filing cabinet that constantly grows, even when I don't want it to."

Ella wanted to go on, but Byford took the lead. "So, you must be familiar with a gentleman named Barry Windham. I believe he retired a few years ago, but he worked at Quanta for a while."

"Barry," Aleister smiled. "He was my favorite. He treated me like a son."

Ella and Byford shared the same expression, a hybrid of suspicion and uncertainty. Each one waited for the other to go in with the killing blow. Byford took charge again. He reached down under the table, pulled out a brown folder and opened it up. He slid a crime scene photo across to the suspect.

"Did he look like this when you knew him?" Byford asked.

Aleister eyed the picture with bewilderment at first. Ella watched him closely for any signs of guilt or detachment or familiarity. The person who committed the murder would react strongly to it, especially considering mistakes were made at the scene. Presenting crime scene photos to suspects was presenting them a challenge.

But this suspect reacted like no other she'd seen before. Aleister Black planted his head on the interrogation room table and began to cry. His sobbing began lightly at first, then grew into violent moans not unlike that of a toddler who'd just broken his best toy.

"Mr. Black, why are you upset?" Byford asked.

Aleister cried for another full minute before sitting back in his chair and shutting his eyes tightly. "He's dead. I can't believe he's dead," Aleister called.

"You knew Mr. Windham, then?" Ella asked. "Please tell us the truth, Aleister. This is very important."

Aleister wiped his face with his sleeve, drenching his arm in various bodily fluids. "I knew Barry very well. He was so good to me. A lot of people at work make fun of me, but Barry was so kind. He always helped me when I needed it. He wanted to train me as an electrician to get me out of the warehouse, but..." Aleister held up his hands for a moment. His right hand twitched violently. "I can't do something like that with my condition."

He cried again, more forcefully this time, shaking his head as though it might undo the reality of Barry's death. His intense cries filled the room and Ella's eardrums, and by the look on Byford's face, even he was beginning to doubt this man's guilt.

"Aleister, we don't think you did this," Ella said. Byford went to interject but Ella quickly grabbed his arm in a *trust me* motion. "Well, to be clear, *I* don't think you did this."

The declaration did nothing to cease the suspect's tears. They came in floods, confirming to Ella that the display in front of her was one of genuine emotion. As far as she was concerned, Aleister Black wasn't their killer. The realization was both disappointing and welcome. This man had enough hardships without being a suspected murderer too.

"Don't you?" he asked finally.

"No. But you need to tell us where you were on the nights of these people's deaths, okay?"

"I can do that," he said between heavy breaths.

"April 27, April 30 and May 1. Between midnight and one am on all of them. Can you do that?"

"At home. On all of them. I promise."

"Can anyone verify that?" asked Ella.

Aleister shook his head as more tears welled up. "No. I live alone. But I might have some gaming logs that prove I was online. Does that count?"

The truth was that it would be a tricky sell in a court of law, but it was better than nothing. "Yes, it would. Anything you have would be great."

"I'll get them. I will. Please catch whoever did this to Barry."

"Trust us," Ella said. "We're sorry you had to find out this way. We're going to leave you in the hands of some other officers now. They'll get you out of here. Will you be okay?"

Aleister looked her in the eye and nodded silently. His crying stopped when he realized his ordeal was coming to an end.

"If you need anything, call the NDPD and ask for Agent Dark, alright?"

The agents left the room and joined Sheriff Hunter on the other side. Ella breathed a heavy sigh, feeling like she'd just stepped out of a boxing ring with a world champion. These interviews chipped away at your soul, she thought. Every time you saw an innocent person grieve, it killed you a little more on the inside.

"If he's an actor, he's a damn good one," the sheriff said.

"I don't think he did this," added Byford. "At first I thought he was our guy, but he's not capable of this. There's no killer instinct there. Just a troubled kid."

Ella rested her forehead against the two-way mirror, observing the broken man inside. She thought about her own problems and wondered

107

how they compared to his. This guy was a loner, mentally struggling and now a murder suspect. To top it off, he'd just found one of the few people who treated him right was dead. Which one of them had it worse, she thought. Him or her?

"Ella, are you alright?" asked Byford. He came up beside her and put his hand on her shoulder. As far as she could remember, it was the first physical contact they'd had.

"Been better, but thank you for asking. Are you okay?"

"Don't worry about me. Why don't you go grab breakfast or something? You look like you need a break."

She wasn't hungry, but a break was welcome. "Good idea. Do you want anything?"

"No, I'm fine. Take your time."

Byford and Hunter took their leave. Two officers unlocked the interrogation room and walked inside. Once again, Aleister cowered like he was about to be tortured by the Spanish Inquisition. Ella suddenly thought of Mia and wondered how she'd have reacted to this suspect. Would she have followed the circumstantial evidence, or would she have analyzed Aleister's outburst of emotion and come to the same conclusion she had?

No, Ella laughed to herself. It wouldn't have gone down that way at all. If Ella knew Mia, and she believed she did, Mia would have known the guy was innocent from the moment she laid eyes on him.

No one with trembling hands like that could make the accurate incisions their killer did.

***

After an hour-long video call with the director, Mia Ripley packed up her things in her Manhattan office and prepared to head home. Melissa, having barely said a word since their ordeal at the gas station, did the same at a much slower pace. Their suspects had been caught by local police.

The director had spent the majority of their call speaking through the cracks in his fingertips. He'd heard about the disaster before Mia even had a chance to tell him; something that always riled Edis up no matter the situation. He'd chewed the agents out like cheap tobacco and even left Melissa in tears. Mia, not so much. She'd seen it all before, but her penalty had been more than she expected: two weeks suspension. In reality, Mia hadn't done a whole lot wrong, but Melissa's actions were hers to own.

Melissa's punishment had been much worse. Mia had explained everything in full detail, much to Melissa's disapproval. From the reluctance to leave her vehicle to shooting a fleeing suspect to causing two-hundred thousand dollars' worth of damages. For all that, Melissa had been relegated back to her desk job. Her career in the field started and ended on the same day.

Mia thought about opposing the decision, but it was for the best in the long run. Melissa didn't have the natural instincts that a field agent needed, she realized. Textbooks couldn't teach you everything. You needed a head on your shoulders to survive in this game. Everyone thought they had it, but it wasn't until you came face to face with real hardships that you discovered whether you really did.

"I'm sorry, Ripley," Melissa said as she hauled her bag over her shoulder. The tears had dried now. "I'm just... in shock. Two hundred thousand dollars. I could have killed people."

There was no point kicking the girl when she was down, Mia thought.

"No one got hurt. And two hundred grand isn't going to bankrupt the Bureau."

"I guess we're lucky."

Lucky, Mia thought. That wasn't the word she'd use right now. "Take it as a lesson. Field work isn't for you."

"I'm gutted. I really wanted to give this a shot."

"You gave it more than a shot," Mia said. She saw the girl's expression resume despair. "Sorry. I didn't mean it like that."

Melissa sulked her way to the door, head down, eyes on the ground. Mia knew they'd both remember this for the rest of their lives, and not for the right reasons. Melissa for nearly blowing up a gas station, Mia for making a string of bad decisions that led to the fact. How had she got so things right with Ella but completely missed the mark with Melissa?

Thinking about it, maybe she was lucky after all.

Mia grabbed the last item standing. Her phone. As she picked it up, she saw the notifications on the screen. Too many to count, but one name stood out to her. The name she'd seen on her phone every day for the past two weeks.

"Speak of the devil and she's sure to appear," Mia said. Another missed call from her old partner.

Melissa turned around. "Huh?"

Mia hadn't realized she'd spoken aloud. "Sorry. Nothing. Can you just wait downstairs? There's one last thing I have to do here."

Melissa waited a second before responding, probably fearing that Mia's task involved her misdemeanor somehow. "Umm, okay. See you down there."

Mia sat back down at her desk and scrolled through all of Ella's messages and missed calls from the past few weeks. Too many to count. Mia sighed, opened up her messages screen, closed it again.

No, it was time. She needed to do it.

This had gone on long enough.

CHAPTER TWENTY

Ella found herself driving through Newark with no particular destination in sight. Dead ends were familiar territory to her now, but it didn't stop them stinging just as hard every single time. Two days, two suspects, two releases. It didn't get any easier.

Maybe through subconscious familiarity, she found she was on the same street as her motel. Might as well get a coffee from her room, she thought. It wouldn't be as nice as franchise outlet coffee, but it would be a lot cheaper. Every case, she doubted her ability to reach the finish line, but that was usually all she doubted. Now, her mounting problems were beginning to suffocate her, and for once, her detective skills were the least of her problems. All morning, she'd felt her phone continually vibrate, and she hadn't dared check the messages because she knew what her reaction would be: anger.

Was it her fault she didn't like her relationship? Did she do something wrong to make Mark react this way to her? Would he be like this if she was different, maybe if she was tall, tanned, and blonde? Well, she wasn't willing to find out, because next time she talked to him, she was giving him the truth: she didn't want to be with him anymore.

She parked her car and went into the motel. She'd get coffee from the room, she decided, plus she could get her phone charger. With the influx of messages, it must be close to dead. She checked her battery level and saw it was at eleven percent, but as she did, she noticed the barrage of notifications on her home screen. Seven messages from Mark, two missed calls, and one message from a name she never expected to see again.

Mia Ripley had replied to her. Ella saw her name, felt the joy, and tapped into her message as she stood on the motel stairs.

Then dread returned, pushing her further down into despair.

Please stop trying to contact me.

Right then, Ella could have curled up into a ball and slept forever. She felt like she'd lost her place in the world, like she was fighting a stream of constant, growing, never-ending battles that she didn't want or need in her life.

First there was this unsub. Someone out there, someone who she could have already walked past on the street, was systematically killing off people in the coin collecting trade. Every time a new body showed up, the blood was on her hands. It was her responsibility to stop this maniac, and even with three crime scenes, three dead bodies and a solid link between them all, her case was still directionless at the moment.

Then there was Mark, the man who'd shown such promise upon their first meeting only to morph into an insecure, jealous monster at the mere mention of another man's name. It wasn't normal. Her ex-boyfriends didn't do that. Her friends' boyfriends didn't do that. No man or woman should do that. It was what the young folk called *toxic behavior* according to her late-night Googling.

Now Mia, the woman who gave her this job in the first place, an opportunity few people would ever get, despised her. Ella deserved some backlash from her actions. Of that, she was more than happy to admit. She wished no ill will towards Mia for acting the way she did. More so than anything else, Ella hated herself for being so short-sighted throughout the whole ordeal.

She pulled out her keycard and opened her motel door. The coffee sachets looked tempting, but the bed looked better. She wanted to collapse on it, sleep for a few days and wake up to a solved case. No more death, no more bodies, no more coins. Just the bliss and stress-free living that she suddenly craved. Maybe it was time to go back to Intelligence and stay there, resume her life of minimal responsibilities and maybe get her kicks through rock climbing and martial arts tournaments.

It wasn't until she sat on the bed and organized her thoughts that she remembered the note. The note sitting on her nightstand, possibly sent to her by the country's most sadistic serial killer. She tried not to look at it, but her peripheral vision betrayed her intentions. Through some bizarre mechanism of her cognitive system, the note looked longer, wider in her fringe vision. She gave up, deciding to embrace the dread, turned around and looked at it.

The note looked longer because there was another next to it.

Ella begged it to be a product of her stress. Or one was the letter, one was the envelope. She edged closer to the nightstand, finding two envelopes sitting side by side.

Her stomach tied in knots, and she had to swallow hard to keep the bile from rising to her throat. How did this get here? Had the maid moved it? Had someone been in her room? How the hell was this possible? Just as she reached out to grab it, a gentle knock at the door rose the hairs on her neck. Ella was off the bed and holding her pistol in the weaver stance in a single movement. She edged closer to the door, peered through the spyhole and saw a familiar face standing on the other side. She lowered her weapon and opened the door.

"Nigel?" she asked. "Is everything alright? I was just getting a coffee."

Nigel held her stare for a few seconds, the most he'd done in the past two days. "No, you weren't," he said.

"Huh? I was. I swear."

"Can I come in?" he asked.

This all seemed incredibly uncharacteristic of him. What was going on here? She looked back at her room, quickly scanning to make sure it was presentable. "Okay, but why?"

Byford walked past her and took a seat at the dressing table. "Shut the door, please."

Ella did as he asked, slowly walked back to the room and perched herself on the end of the bed. "Nigel, what's going on? I'm worried."

"Don't be. In fact, that's part of the problem. I might be new to this job, but I know a struggling agent when I see one. Ella, you're having a hard time, aren't you?"

Ella became flustered; her face turned red. She didn't know whether to go for brutal honesty or modest insincerity. She was more taken aback by the sudden change in Byford's demeanor.

"Yes, I am. Is it obvious?"

"Not to most people, but I've been trained to spot distress. You exhibit all the classic signs. Do you want to tell me what's wrong and I'll see if I can help? Working serial cases is hard enough, and even harder with a stressed partner."

"You want the short version? Everything is going wrong. Work, relationships, this case, everything. It's all come at once, like some grief tsunami."

Byford leaned forward in the chair. "And the long version?"

Ella laughed. "That would take a long time."

"You'd be surprised how minuscule your problems are in the grand scheme of things. Relationships, let's start there. Problems with your husband, boyfriend, girlfriend?"

"Boyfriend." There was that word again. "We've only been seeing each other two weeks, but basically, he doesn't trust me. When I told him I was partnered with a man, he flipped."

"Wow, it's been a long time since I've been *the other guy*. I'm guessing from that statement he hasn't seen my face?" Byford laughed. It was the first time Ella had seen anything but a straight expression on his face.

"He might have. I don't know. It's Mark Balzano."

"Mark is your boyfriend? I know him. A fine agent, but not great boyfriend material. Do you love him?"

"No. Not even close." Ella surprised herself with how easy it was to declare such a thing.

"Then you know what you have to do. And if he's borderline abusive, you need to do it soon."

"Break it off," Ella said.

"Yup. When people show you who they really are, believe them. Now, this case, what's the issue?"

"Isn't it obvious? We're nowhere close to the finish line."

"So? We'll keep working until it is. It's as easy as that. Just because you've solved cases in a week, doesn't mean they'll all go that route. It took us ten years to track down Bin Laden."

Usually, Ella hated condensing solutions down to a single sentence, but in this case, it seemed to work. Byford was right. All they could really do was carry on.

"True. I mean, it's obvious, but you're right."

"Sometimes you just need someone else to say the words. Now, what else about work is getting you down? I've been with the FBI for fifteen years, so I've seen it all. Been there, done that."

Here came the tricky part. Ella didn't know whether she really wanted to drag Byford into this world of troubles. Besides, Mia wouldn't be too pleased if Ella went round telling people about their falling out.

"Me and my ex-partner. FBI partner. I went behind her back and did something I shouldn't have. That's why I'm with you and not her."

"Do you want to talk about what you did?"

"I visited someone she didn't want me to, and I didn't tell her. She found out through the other person, then everything went to hell."

Byford looked unimpressed. "Big deal. And this was Agent Ripley?"

"It was."

"Well, I can't speak for her, but it sounds like you're both being overdramatic here. You probably shouldn't have done that, but at the same time, she should really give you a chance to apologize. Has she done that?"

"No. She hasn't."

"Then she's being unfair. This isn't all on you. You made a mistake. Shit happens."

Ella welcomed the suggestion that she wasn't the bad guy in this scenario. She wasn't perfect, but neither was the other person involved. "Thank you for the encouragement. But Mia breaking it off with me felt like the ultimate failure, like I'd let her down. It was the one thing I didn't want to do, but I got tangled up in this web and things just got worse and worse. You know?"

Byford adjusted his chair then sat forward again. "Oh, I do know. Remember the other day, you asked me why I left counter-terrorism?"

Ella recalled their conversation in the back of the cab. "I do."

"Here's the story. You might feel better afterwards. So, there I am, about three years ago, I wake up to a phone call in the middle of the night from the director. He wants me in England immediately. A religious fanatic with an assault rifle has taken twenty-four hostages in a grocery store. Been there for two days already and the British police didn't have the skillset they needed. So I jump on a plane, and the entire ride there I'm trying to figure this guy out. What does he want? How can I talk him down? This whole scene was nothing new to me, so I was pretty confident I could talk the hostages out of there."

Ella listened closely. Finally, she was getting a glimpse of the person, not just the career.

"I get there and I'm talking on the phone to the gunman. I give him what he wants, which is status. He wanted to be mentioned in the same leagues as the major terrorists, so I tell him he's got the whole country paralyzed with fear. I tell him that if he comes out now, he won't spend his life in jail, but he will if any lives are lost. We come to a deal, and that deal was I meet him at the door, and he gives me his weapon."

Ella put herself in the situation. She wouldn't know what to do for the best. She couldn't imagine playing such a crucial role in the lives of so many.

"So I've got about a thousand people watching. The cops, the press, even the Prime Minister of England. I go to the door, open it up and that's when I see this terrorist just standing there, laughing. I realize right then and there that it's all over. That's the moment my whole being shatters and never mends. My career is over, my mind is broken, and there's a good chance my life is too."

"Why? What happened?"

"I watched the target gun down everybody in that store right in front of me. I'll never forget the terror on their faces when they realized what was about to happen. Paralyzing fear, acceptance of death. The gunman unloaded on the hostages and as fast as I was, I wasn't any match for burst fire from a Beretta 93R. Seven people died before I managed to stop him. Blood washed down the aisles, body parts rained on me. I still see the massacre to this day whenever I go to sleep. I know I'll never escape it."

"Holy s... that was *you?*" Ella said, her jaw hanging low. She remembered the case very well but had no idea Byford was involved. Byford was manipulated by a terrorist to watch mass slaughter. There were no words in the English language to comfort him. "Sorry. That's just..."

"Unforgivable," he said, "I know. I'll never forgive myself for it. It eats me up, day after day. I took a year off. Had to go through extensive counseling, but I learned to live with it. Harness the contempt I hold for myself and use it to make the world a better place for others. Sorry I had to get so dark, but I hope that puts your own problems into perspective. You talked to someone your partner didn't like. The grown woman will get over it, alright? Now how about we get a coffee, get back to work and stop this son of a bitch before he kills anyone else, yes?"

She suddenly felt like kind of a jerk for judging Byford so readily. The man had been through a war, lived to tell the tale and dealt with the trauma like a soldier. He didn't cower or retreat into a hidey-hole for the rest of his life. He took responsibility, Ella realized. That was what she had to do.

"Hell yes," Ella said, rising to her feet. "Let's do this thing. That was a brutal story, but you've helped me put things in perspective. Thank you for coming."

"Any time, partner. I'll let you sort yourself out. Meet you downstairs when you're done." Byford jumped out of his chair and left the room. Ella took a moment to herself, processing the past ten minutes in silence. She went to the bathroom mirror, threw some water on her face then checked her reflection. Not great, but there were more important things to worry about than how she looked. Back in the bedroom, she saw the letters again, realizing now that she hadn't even read the second letter.

She grabbed it, pulled it out of the envelope and saw the same ink, same handwriting.

I'LL SEE YOU SOON.

This time, it didn't scare her. It didn't faze her at all. She grabbed the other letter, crumpled them both up and threw them in the trash.

116

"Yes, you will see me soon, you piece of shit," she said as she walked out the door.

CHAPTER TWENTY ONE

Across their office table, Byford looked different now, like he had something substantial behind that corporate exterior. Ella had arrived at the precinct with new determination to break this case open, so her first point of call was research. Something in her copious notes would give them a direction to explore; she and Byford just had to find it.

"Where to start?" asked Byford. "You got us this far, so consider me your servant."

"Please, don't say that. We're equal. You've played your part too. Have any new reports come in that we can take a look at?"

Byford organized his paperwork. He pulled out two new sheets. "These came in while you were gone. The sheriff got an expert in to appraise all of the coins. Here's what he found." He pushed the papers over to Ella's side of the desk. She read them through.

"So, nothing particularly rare here then. Middle-of-the-road value too."

"Yeah. Have you noticed that they increase in value with every crime scene? The Kennedy nickels are pretty much worthless, the yens are worth about twenty dollars each, and the Chinese coins are about fifty."

Ella saw the same pattern. "Interesting. It suggests our killer is evolving. Or that he's targeting his victims in terms of importance." The next section of the report stated that the coins could have come from a countless number of sources, so tracking them back through previous owners would be impossible.

"I think we need to go further into this world of coin collecting," said Byford. "What if we went through the police archives and found any crime that involves coins or money or debt. Then we could cross-check their names against the people in coin collecting communities."

Ella liked the optimism, but the suggested task was a massive undertaking. "Local officers did that yesterday. The results ran into multiple thousands. Plus, with how many coin collectors there are in Newark alone, even narrowing it down by known collectors' names would yield too many results to sift through. It's a great idea, but we'd need some manpower."

Ella's phone flashed up. For once, it wasn't from Mark. It was a notification that her takeout coffees had arrived. "Back in a second. Breakfast is here."

She left the office, went through the open-plan area of the office, and down the steps to the foyer. She opened the door and collected her order from the deliveryman. Just before she closed the door, she heard a voice.

"Miss Dark?"

Ella peered around the door. Standing against the outside wall was Aleister Black. He appeared to be shuffling back and forth as he gripped his forearm with the opposite hand. Ella recognized the signs immediately. Overbearing anxiety. Withholding a secret, maybe.

"Aleister. Are you okay? What are you still doing here?" She put her coffees down and joined him outside.

"I was on my way home, but I came back."

His face was a wreck. He looked like he'd been through the wars. "Why? You need to go and rest."

"I had something I wanted to tell you. It's only something small, but I thought you better know."

Ella's curiosity piqued. "Of course. I'm listening. Please say whatever's on your mind."

"You mentioned that you found an Okinawa 1964 coin alongside Jimmy's body, didn't you?"

"Yes, we did. Gold. One thousand yen."

"Those parts aren't important. What's important is the year. It's always about the year. Forget everything else about the coins. Focus on the year."

Ella raised her eyebrows. As far as she knew, Aleister wasn't aware the other coins were also from 1964. "Is that symbolic of something?"

"No," Aleister shook his head. "But if your killer is also a coin collector, then he was born in 1964."

Ella checked their surroundings to make sure no one was within earshot. "What do you mean? Why do you think that?" she asked.

"It's the collector mindset. It might not make sense to regular people, but every collector has what we call a special interest inside their own collecting niche. For me, it's Soviet coins. Others might focus on wartime coins. But for most collectors, especially older generations, it's the year of their birth. I think it's his way of leaving something *of himself* at each scene. Collectors are naturally possessive people. They like to boast of the things they own."

Now that she'd heard it from someone else's mouth, it seemed obvious. She was so focused on thinking the coins were symbolic to each victim that she didn't stop to think the coins might be symbolic to the unsub. If the killer was born in 1964, that would make him 57 years old. Based on the sneak attacks, she'd profiled the killer to be young and agile, but was it really so necessary that he was? Why couldn't an older male pull off the same level of cunning?

"Aleister, thank you so much," she said. She reached out and hugged him, hoping such affection might lessen his sense of vulnerability. Even though she couldn't see his expression, she sensed his awkwardness.

"I have to go," he said. "I need to go to work."

Aleister disappeared down the street, and Ella returned to her office. She pulsed with so much excitement she forgot to pick her coffee back up. She vaulted up the stairs, through the precinct and back into her office.

"Nigel," Ella said as she arrived back. "Let's do your idea. Can we get the records of every crime relating to coins or debt in the past twenty years?"

"Woah," Byford said, "hold on a minute. You said that would take too long."

"I did, but I'm backtracking. It's a good idea and I know how we can narrow it down."

Byford clicked away on his laptop. "I've still got the save file the sheriff sent me. I can execute it again. How do we narrow it down?"

Ella hunched over Byford's screen as he navigated for the file. "Aleister just caught me while I was outside."

"He's still here?"

"He went and came back, but he told me that a lot of coin collectors obtain mint sets from their birth years, especially older ones. He said that our unsub must be born in 1964. He said it was something to do with the collector mindset. But to be honest, I think there's another reason Aleister thought that."

"Because that's what Aleister would do if he was this killer," Byford said.

It was like he read her mind. "Exactly what went through my head."

"Maybe we are in sync after all. Here are the results."

Endless columns of data flashed up Byford's laptop, all in text barely big enough to comprehend. The tally in the bottom left corner said there were 3,426 results. "That's a lot, but let's break it down by perpetrators born in 1964."

Byford scrolled around the screen looking for the filter options. "Your patience is required," he said. "I don't know this system. There, found you." He typed in the information.

The 3,426 reduced to 32. The results showed crimes that involved coins, however minimal or trivial. It could have been crimes committed for financial gain or a pensioner beaten to death with a bag of pennies. Ella wasn't going to dive into each individual case until she was sure they'd exhausted all their filter options.

"Better, but still a lot. How can we narrow it down further?" Byford asked.

"We're looking for a white male who lives or works within ten miles of the first crime scene. Zip code 19711. An unsub like this wouldn't stray far away from familiar territory, especially for his first murder."

Byford followed Ella's lead. "Done. Any more?" Thirteen results disappeared, leaving 19 in place.

"He would have started small, minor issues like disorderly behavior. He may have been diagnosed with mental health issues from a young age."

Byford ticked and unticked boxes, filled in keywords and clicked around the database with painful slowness. "Sorry I'm taking my time. I don't want to screw this up." He clicked the execute button and the results dropped to 3. "Bang, and the dirt is gone," he exclaimed.

Three. That was as good as it was going to get, Ella thought. It would be different if she was divulging a simple psychological profile for a recent murder, but she was looking for crimes that had been committed any time in the past two decades. It made it all the more difficult to determine the necessary filters.

"Let's dive in. What's the first one?"

Byford pulled up the first name and read the notes. "Vincent Jones. He killed a woman in the street and stole a quarter from her purse. This was in 2006."

"Not our man. Our killer is only targeting men, plus he stole something from the scene rather than leaving something behind."

Byford clicked off and went into the next name. "Adrian Neville. 2011. Killed a man by accident when he flicked a quarter off the top of River Tower. Definitely not," Byford said and clicked back.

Ella's breathing doubled in speed. Last name on the list. If this wasn't a hit, it was back to the drawing board. "Final contestant, come on down."

Byford loaded up the screen. The first words Ella saw were *suspected homicide.*

"Hey, this is more like it," said Byford. "I think we could have something."

Ella glided through the report, forming a picture of this potential suspect in a matter of seconds. His name was Kevin Steen, but he was a different category of criminal from the other suspects.

"Goddamn. He's a professional thief," Ella said.

"Looks damn well like it. Check this part out." Byford moved his cursor. "He burglarized an antique shop in 2016. Then a few days later, the owner was murdered. Pretty suspicious."

"You're not kidding. Looks like he only stole rare coins too. Can you check his last known whereabouts?"

Byford dug into Steen's current status. "He was in prison for robbery until...," he stopped mid-sentence. Ella finished it for him.

"Last month." They exchanged a look that said the same thing. "Holy crap. We need to check with this guy's parole officer. Can you get his details?"

"One sec," Byford said. Ella grabbed her phone and opened up her keypad. Byford read out the number she needed. Ella dialed it.

One ring.

Two.

"Hello, Community Services Probation and Aftercare, Julia speaking, how can I help?"

"Hi, my name's Agent Dark with the FBI. I need to speak with a...," Ella glanced at Byford, realizing she hadn't got the officer's name she needed.

"Kathy Starks," Byford mouthed.

"Miss Kathy Starks," Ella repeated. "It's about a parolee under her care."

"One moment please," the receptionist said. The line went silent, then symphonic music fizzled through. The volume dynamic was completely off.

Another voice joined the line a second later. "Hello, this is P.O. Starks."

"Hi, Miss Starks," Ella side. "My name's Agent Dark with the FBI, designation C131. May I talk with you about a parolee of yours named Kevin Steen?"

"Mr. Steen is currently missing, Agent. Do you have information on his whereabouts?"

"Missing?" she asked. She directed the comment towards Byford as much as her new friend on the phone.

"Yes Agent, Mr. Steen didn't report for his last parole check. We've attempted to track him down with no success. What is it you need to know?"

"We believe Mr. Steen may be responsible for a series of murders throughout Newark. Do you believe he would be capable of that?"

Kathy Starks hesitated for a moment. "I'm afraid I couldn't comment in a professional capacity. Could you do me a small favor, please Agent Dark? Could you call me on my cell phone? I'm having trouble hearing you down this line."

"Okay. I can do that."

Kathy recited the number then hung up. Ella dialed the new number as she looked at Nigel in confusion.

"Weird. She asked me to call her cell," Ella said.

"Did she say he was missing?" Byford asked.

Her call connected. The same voice picked up on the other side. "Hello, Agent Dark?"

"Hi, can you hear me better now?"

"Miss Dark, sorry to have to do that. Truthfully, I heard you fine on the other line, but I needed to talk to you off the record. I can't do that on my work line."

Ella's curiosity surged to uncontrollable levels. "Off the record? Sure, but why?"

"Professional courtesy prevents me from speculating and doing so can cost me my job. But you said Kevin Steen is a suspect in a murder case?"

"He is, yes. Three murders." Ella heard Kathy sigh desperately down the phone, like she was struggling to control her breathing. Her voice lowered to a whisper.

"Kevin Steen is a notorious thief, but he's also highly dangerous. I assume you know about his past."

"I know he was in prison for thievery."

"He was tried for the murder of the same store owner but acquitted due to lack of evidence. But in private talks with me, Kevin more or less admitted he did it."

Ella waved to get Byford's attention. She flailed her arm around in a futile attempt to relay the conversation. "Really? He admitted it?"

"If you ask me, yes. But it doesn't stop there. During our last contact, he told me he 'had big plans.' I didn't know what he was talking about. I thought he was just being his usual grandiose self. But he said he was going after 'the big four,' and he was going to do it in the span of a week."

"The big four?" Ella said. "Any ideas what that meant?"

"None. I thought it was just Kevin being Kevin. Talking about turning his life around, maybe. Then I saw the news of Alan Yates and Jimmy Loveridge and my heart just sank."

Ella digested the information, tried to process it all and make sense of it. "Hang on a second, why did you assume Kevin Steen had anything to do with their deaths?" She detected Kathy's hesitance, despite them being a hundred miles apart. The line crackled with static.

"We are off the record, yes? This information can't be used in a court of law."

"No, I promise."

"Well, this is by no means confirmed. It's just one of those rumors, one perpetuated by Kevin himself."

"I'm listening."

"Alan Yates and Jimmy Loveridge. Kevin Steen was their *supplier*. He would burglarize items for them. How do you think they both made so much money?"

"Oh, Christ. That's… very helpful," Ella said. "Do you know where Kevin might be now?"

"No. We've had police searching for him for several days. He was due to check in on April 26 but never did."

Ella turned to the timeline on the whiteboard. That was the day before the first murder. Something was going on here.

"Thank you, Miss Starks."

"You're welcome. Please don't mention this conversation in any official capacity."

Ella understood the need. "Trust me. One last thing before you go. Does the name Barry Windham mean anything to you?" She heard a tapping down the other end of the line.

"Windham, Windham," Kathy repeated. "Yes, but…"

Kathy stopped. Ella sensed a reveal was forthcoming. "You know it?"

"I just checked Kevin's notes. The store owner who Kevin was suspected of killing. He was Barry Windham's brother."

That's it, Ella thought, finally seeing a clear picture for the first time. Everything fell into place, like a million-piece jigsaw that had been scattered across Newark. The revelation brought a euphoric high that nothing in the world could match.

"Thank you for your help. You might have just helped us find a murderer." Ella hung up, turned to Byford and didn't know where to start.

This killer is clearing up loose ends, she repeated.

CHAPTER TWENTY TWO

They always returned home. It didn't matter if they were petty criminals or wanted fugitives. If they were on the run, the one place they'd visit again would be their home. That's why Ella was sat in a car one hundred yards from the house of Kevin Steen, eyes glued to it like a hawk. The building was a split-level home, with a set of wooden steps leading to the front door. Cream window blinds obscured the interior, and between them and the single-hung windows sat a row of potted plants. Not exactly how she pictured the home of a notorious thief. She and Byford now entered their third hour of waiting.

"Ella, this is great and everything, but we can't sit here all day," Byford said.

She was starting to feel the same way. Steen would return eventually, but it could be days or weeks before he did. Career criminals had places they could hide long-term. "Yeah, you're right. What do you wanna do?"

"What if I patrol the streets? I'll get some of the local PD to come with me. We can cover more ground that way."

"Sounds like a plan. If you catch a whiff of this guy, buzz me straight away."

"Same. If he comes home, call for backup. Don't try and take this guy down on your own." Byford pulled out his phone and made a quick call back to the precinct. "I'm gonna jump in a squad car down the road. We'll stay within a few miles."

Byford exited the car and disappeared down the road, leaving Ella alone. She'd looked at the house for so long now that the image was burned into her retinas. She had every exterior detail committed to memory so if anything changed when she blinked, she'd know about it.

Ella considered the suspect and how his thought process might be operating. Kevin Steen had a connection to each victim and a motive to kill them. Ella put herself in his head and ran through the events of the past five years. In 2016, Kevin Steen burglarized Gold Rush Coins in Wilmington, Delaware. Steen was caught in the act by the store owner but managed to flee. Three days later, the store owner wound up dead.

Steen was tried for the crime and ultimately found innocent of murder, but such an ordeal would take its toll on the man. He'd harbor resentment for the man who caught him and put him through a lengthy trial process, so after that, could Steen be targeting the people from his past? If these rumors were true of Steen supplying goods to people around Newark, what triggered him to take their lives? Was he trying to wipe the slate clean, or maybe exact vengeance upon people who used him?

And who were the "big four" he allegedly spoke of? Four victims, four people from his past? If that was the case, that meant he could be planning to strike tonight. A deranged mind like this would be thirsty for retribution after the mistakes he made with Barry Windham last night. Right now, he'd be doubting himself, and the only way to make things better would be to pull off a flawless crime scene like the first two.

Ella's phone vibrated on the dashboard, and for the umpteenth time today, Mark's name appeared. She didn't read the messages because they'd just upset her. She didn't have time to deal with an insecure, emotionally stunted abuser when there were more pressing matters to attend to. When she got back to D.C., God knows when, she was going to tell Mark the straight facts. *Our relationship is over.* He'd know the reasons why, and she would be under no obligation to state them even if he begged her to. She owed the man nothing, and she'd start and stop at exactly that.

It was nearing two pm and the rays of spring beamed through her windshield. She welcomed the warmth, then pushed back her car seat so she had ample space to stretch her joints. Her shoulders cracked loudly then she slumped back down in her seat. She shut her eyes, hoping that a minute of micro-sleep might tackle her exhaustion.

Even behind her eyelids she saw the house. A fantasy scenario of how her meeting with Kevin Steen might play out looped in her mind, then she shot awake, craving the meeting for real. She pushed the exhaustion to one side, kept her eyes glued on the house and only blinked when she really needed to.

It was going to be a long day.

***

Ella glanced over at the dashboard clock. Nearly two hours had passed, and everything was still the same. A row of houses, an empty street, and nothing in Steen's house had changed.

One time when she was working for the Virginia Police Department, an officer had told her that chasing down criminals made up one percent of a cop's job. The other ninety-nine percent was spent staring at people's houses. That ninety-nine percent, he said, was why so many cops killed themselves. She thought he was joking, but actually doing the task painted his comments in a different light.

No missed calls from Byford. No messages from Mark, for a change. She began to feel like time was running out here, and she couldn't risk wasting time for fear of another life being lost. In the past three and a half hours, only two pedestrians had walked past. This was an optimistic task, but a lost cause given the urgency.

Ella put her key in the ignition and flipped it once. She studied her surroundings one more time. She no longer saw this street as an animated, tangible part of the world she lived in, rather a two-dimensional backdrop hung up at the rear of the stage where her life story played out.

But then something came to her. A note of irregularity. She saw movement where she hadn't before.

Someone was outside Kevin Steen's house. Going through the gate. Pushing a key into the door.

Ella fired out of her seat with the speed of a cheetah. She softly closed the car door as not to alert the man to her presence. She couldn't make out his features so wasn't sure if it was the suspect or not, but who else would be venturing into his home?

She crossed the road, noticing that the door was left wide open. From that, she could only deduce that whoever had arrived wasn't planning on staying long. She thought of the times she'd forgotten her purse and had to run back to her apartment: in, leave door open, out again in seconds. It saved messing around with the latches.

Ella quickly one-rung her partner. There was no time to chat. He'd know what she meant. She gripped her pistol and handcuffs and swooped towards the house, making her way silently to the still-open front door. She caught her first glimpse of the interior and was impressed by the little she saw. She never expected a thief to have such good taste. She stood ready for battle, put her racing thoughts to rest, then pushed the door open.

On the other side, something stopped its momentum. Then like a ghostly apparition, Kevin Steen appeared in front of her. He looked much different than his police mugshot. He was 57 years old but looked older, with a shaved head, deep brown eyes, and thin pink lips. Ella saw a scrawny physique beneath his beige trousers and white jacket.

Kevin gave no introduction, simply went about his business as though she didn't exist.

"Mr. Steen?" she asked. She caught his eye for a second, then he stepped outside his house and tried to slam his door shut. Ella wedged her foot in the gap, eager to see the contents of his house. Somewhere in there would be evidence of his crimes. Steen walked off down the pathway.

"Kevin," she shouted. "I'm with the FBI. Please stay where you are."

Kevin did not comply; he turned the corner out of his house and started up the pathway. Ella jumped over the small fence and cut him off at the pass. "Kevin, we need to speak with you," she said as she showed him her badge.

Then the suspect froze. He checked his phone and turned in the other direction. Ella ran after him, caught up and grabbed him by the wrist. Kevin Steen spun to face her, bringing his nose right up against hers.

"You stay out of this, little woman. You hear?"

His voice was rough and gravelly like his vocal cords had charred to flakes. Her face against his, she didn't blink or twitch or move.

"Kevin, you've got three seconds to start talking, and I suggest you do it."

He pushed up against her. A classic intimidation tactic. The force displaced her balance, but she kept upright. Ella had seen it a million times.

"Trust me. You don't want any of this. Go home. This never happened."

"Wanna tell me who the big four are?"

Steen's lips arched down at the edges. He sniffed violently then spat in Ella's face. At her moment of disorientation, she heard footsteps escape from her. She wiped the residue from her eyes then saw Steen running back towards his house. Ella took chase, leaping over the fence and barging shoulder-first into the door. It slammed shut the micro-second she connected with it. It shook on its hinges but stayed firmly in place.

Her brief interaction had confirmed one thing. Kevin Steen was guilty of something.

Ella took two steps back and booted the door with everything she had. It flung open, breaking in two places. Ella leaped inside the home and found herself in the lounge with no sign of a suspect anywhere. She listened for any signs of life but caught nothing.

She ran through the downstairs area, familiarizing herself with the layout and looking for any places where Kevin might hide from her. He'd run back in here for a reason, and something told her she'd quickly find out what it was.

The back door leading to the garden. Locked. All the sizeable windows. Locked. Kevin must be somewhere in here. He couldn't have gotten outside so suddenly.

Ella withdrew her pistol and held the weaver stance as she turned into the hallway.

"Kevin, make yourself known. That's an order," she shouted, expecting nothing by way of reply. From the hallway, she moved up the staircase. At the top, she found four closed doors. Without hesitation, she booted the first one and found a completely barren room. Next in line was the bathroom. Empty with no places to hide.

She raised her foot to take the third door but stopped when she heard a noise. *Tap tap.* Then a scratching sound. She looked up and saw an attic, its cord swaying with life.

Ella wasted no time pulling it down. A wooden staircase toppled down, and Ella had to jump back to avoid it. There was no disguising her invasion, so Ella decided to own it.

"Yield now, Kevin, and I won't shoot," she shouted as she ascended to the peak of the house. A glass roof panel let in just enough light to make out the shape of the room.

"Kevin, I know you're up here. Come out now. You're not getting out."

Wooden boards creaked beneath her feet as she checked the corners. Back to the wall, pistol jumping between the darkened parts of the room. There was a stash of crates in one corner, a pile of bags in the other. She edged along the wall, coming to the third corner, then heard a clink beneath her boot.

Ella glanced down and saw a shining silver coin reflecting back at her. Not one she recognized. An imported one.

Suddenly, she found herself lowering down to it. Not of her own free will, but by an absence of it. A forceful blow to the back of her skull sent her downward and she found herself eye-to-eye with the face on the coin. Her first instinct was to grip her pistol to ensure it stayed put, but a heavy boot to her wrist unlocked her clenched hand. Her attacker kicked the pistol out of reach, rolled her over and clasped his hand around her neck. She felt his fingernails dig into her flesh to the point it drew blood.

The lack of oxygen clouded her ability to think but muscle memory took over in response. Ella wrapped her legs around Steen's mid-section, aiming for either side of the ribs. She squeezed with fury, rolled back on herself and flipped Steen head-first into the crates. She scrambled to her feet, lunged for her weapon.

Got it.

"Don't you dare move," she shouted, training her pistol at Steen's legs. He lay against the crates clutching his forehead. When his arms fell free, Ella saw the massive gash. "Looks painful. But not as painful as having your throat slit, I bet."

"What?" Steen shouted. "The fuck do you want with me, anyway?"

"I want you to empty your pockets. Show me you're unarmed."

"Bitch you've got a gun. If I had a gun, I'd have used it by now."

"Do it."

Steen reached into his jeans and showed his pockets were empty.

"Jacket too."

Steen slowly removed it and slid it across the floor to Ella. "There. Check yourself."

"Alright. Move an inch and I'll make that gash much worse." She bent down without taking her eyes off the suspect, reached into both jacket pockets, and found nothing. She rummaged around the inside and found another.

Her fingertips connected with something.

"What's this, huh," she said. She pinched it between her fingers and extracted it, and when she saw it, her trained target faltered just a little. "Oh my God," she said.

It was two foreign coins wrapped in plastic.

Steen had a lot of explaining to do.

Ella inspected them a little more closely, and as she averted her eyes off the fallen suspect, she saw a blur in her peripheral vision. Footsteps thundered across the floorboards. Ella dropped the coins and re-aimed her pistol at the fleeing suspect but couldn't get a lock-on. To her sheer astonishment, Steen was heading in the opposite direction to the exit. The bizarre direction choice confused her, until Steen seemingly flew towards the ceiling and out the open window. His full weight crashed down the roof outside, sounding like the god of thunder had come to a side street in Newark. She heard the thuds cascade down the roof then suddenly stop.

Ella followed his trail, climbing halfway out of the window to see Kevin Steen standing in place at his garden gate.

Standing opposite him was Agent Byford, gun in hand.

Ella made her way down in haste, bringing the coins down with her. At last, the game was over.

CHAPTER TWENTY THREE

After taking an hour to process everything, Ella went down to the holding cells at the NDPD precinct. Inside, notorious thief Kevin Steen awaited his official arrest. Byford accompanied her down there for their first interview with the suspect.

A uniformed officer unlocked the massive steel door leading into the holding cells. The area was not a pretty affair, not too dissimilar to the jail cells in Ella's strange Victorian dream. A powdery light sifted through the windows. Overhead was a vaulted ceiling, at least thirty feet high, and on it, Ella saw three layers of paint, each a dismal attempt at cheerfulness. The remains of a pair of rusted chains, bolted to the wall, lay on the ground like dead snakes.

"Hello, Kevin," Ella said to the prisoner. He sat on a bench with a bucket of water beside him, gradually applying splashes to his head wound. "Now are you ready to talk?"

"Let's get this over with," he said.

The guard brought two chairs over for the agents. They took a seat outside Steen's cell.

"So, you're a thief. Is that right?"

"I'm whatever pays me."

"Sure. Now, we talked with your parole officer today. Want to tell us why you didn't report to your last check-in?"

Steen shrugged then laughed. "I've been busy. I guess I forgot."

"What could possibly be more important than *not* going back to prison?" asked Byford.

"Look, I've been a free man for a month. Man's got things to do, alright? Tell the bitch I'll call her when I've got five minutes."

"You certainly do have things to do. I'm guessing you've got some old friends to catch up with, right?"

"Something like that," Steen grunted.

"Old friends like Alan Yates, or Jimmy Loveridge."

Steen soared to his feet and gripped the bars of his cell. "I know where this is going, and I didn't touch those bastards. Yeah, I know those guys, but I didn't cut them up."

133

"Are you sure about that?" Byford asked.

"Positive, buddy."

"How do you know them?" asked Ella.

Steen cracked a smile, showing two rows of alarmingly white teeth. Ella remembered reading it was quite common in newly released prisoners because brushing teeth took away hunger pangs.

"I'm a burglar, okay? I've been burgling since I was at my mother's teat, and I'm still going even when I'm at *your* mother's teat. If you want to stay in this game, you gotta put some beats in between you and your hot property."

Ella pulled a look of perplexity. "Kevin, you're 57. Stop speaking like a rapper and tell us in plain English."

Steen retreated to the back of his cage. "When you lift something, you always sell it to a vendor. You don't go round selling to the public like some clueless dipshit. Vendors will then sell it to other vendors. These are the *beats*, so it never comes back you, comprende?"

"We didn't ask for a lesson in stealing. We asked how you know Alan and Jimmy," Byford said.

"I sold them things I'd lifted. Watches, necklaces, old ass shit for Jimmy's stupid shop. They loved it."

"Did they know it was all," Ella paused, "hot property?"

"Jimmy did. He didn't care. Alan not so much. He thought I imported it."

"Kevin, Alan Yates was a banker and philanthropist. Why would he need you?"

"He didn't need me, but men like that are fuckin" *addicted.* They love seeing the numbers go up. He used to sell my stuff for himself directly. All those hospital wings and park benches – that's my doing."

Ella wasn't sure how much of this was true, but she felt a little dirty if that was the case. Hopefully the truth about Alan Yates's antics wouldn't surface after his death, she thought.

"Okay, and now those two men are dead. Bit of a coincidence, isn't it?" asked Byford.

"Yeah, so?" said Steen. "Why would I kill two people who gave me easy cash?"

A reasonable question thought Ella, but she was convinced there was an answer hiding somewhere.

"Maybe they wronged you. Maybe they didn't petition for your release from jail. Perhaps you're ready to turn over a new life and you wanted to wipe out your past connections?"

Steen splashed his head again, this time soaking his skull in the process. "Ha. You're out of your head, lady. I loved those two guys. I oughta be buying them gold tombstones with the money they made me."

"Money that you don't have anymore," said Ella.

"Yeah, that's a kick in the nuts, but what am I gonna do? Cry about it? No, I'm out there hustling again."

"We can tell," Ella said. "Want to tell us about Barry Windham?"

"Who?"

"Barry Windham. A coin collector and local electrician."

"Never heard that name in my life."

"You know his brother, Trevor."

"Oh," Steen tapped himself on the head. "Yeah, I know Barry. I think."

"Well, we found him dead this morning too. That's three people all who have a connection to you. Pretty damning, wouldn't you say?"

Steen came back to the front bars again. "Lady, you ever heard of statistics? Those three guys probably had links to a million suckers like me. Yatesy did business with any old bastard. Loveridge was as crooked as I am and them Windham boys would sell their mother a timeshare if it made them a buck. Plus, what about all the boys I do business with that are still breathing? You ever think about that?"

An hour ago, Ella was convinced they had their man. But now, doubts were coming thick and fast. Kevin Steen was clearly a piece of work and had skeletons in his closet, but she couldn't definitely say he was responsible for these murders. For a mouthy criminal, he made some good points.

"All of our victims were found with coins at the crime scene. Kevin, you're big in the coin collecting scene, correct?" asked Ella.

Steen shrugged his shoulders. "Maybe. Dying art, these days."

"Then what's that I found in your jacket? Something for your personal collection?"

Steen ran his hands across his scalp, spreading some of the drying blood. "I lifted it for a collector. And before you ask, he's not from around here. He lives in New Jersey."

"You want to tell us about this *big four?*" Ella asked. "Your parole officer mentioned it."

"She did, huh? Well, I'm just gonna be honest here because I don't got the energy for this. The big four are the four items you need to get back in the game. I've only been out the pen for a month and I need to get back into it."

"What items are these?" Byford asked.

"Doesn't matter. Anything. It's a thief's term. Most new fences won't accept your goods 'til you've got four valuable pieces. That's how they know you're a big deal and not some schmuck who got lucky."

Ella folded her arms and ran through all of the other questions she had, realizing that Kevin would just deflect them like he had done. She turned to Byford, who looked equally at a loss. If she wanted something from him, she had to dig into his psyche. Rile him up. Mia's old trick.

"Kevin, before we go, mind telling us about your murder trial?"

"No."

"Well, can I make an assumption then?"

"Sure, why not."

"My assumption is that the serial killer I'm looking for is standing right in front of me. We've got enough evidence to send you right back to prison today and make sure you never see daylight again. I think not only did you kill Alan, Jimmy, and Barry, but you killed Barry's brother five years ago too."

Steen dipped his hand on the bucket and violently threw water on his face. He spat a wad out.

"I think you burglarized Trevor's store, then went back and killed the poor old man three days later. Because you're a coward who wants to swipe your problems under the carpet. You couldn't handle a fair fight with him, just like you ambushed me from behind earlier today. You're weak, disgraceful, and hide behind a tough façade."

"Oh yeah? You think?" Steen spat. "We'll see about that."

"Yes, we will. You got a taste of murder five years ago, and you've spent every day since pleasuring yourself to the thought of it. It's the only way a weakling like you can get your kicks. Once you got out, you went back straight back to killing, probably to claw back a sense of dominance after all the late-night beatings you took inside."

"Enough," Steen shouted as he slammed his hands against the cell. "I didn't kill those three guys, you hear me? I steal, I don't kill. Mistakes happen. But I don't kill."

Ella saw the chink in the armor. "Mistakes happen?"

Steen's pupils dilated in fear. He must have realized what he'd said.

"Just tell us the truth, Kevin. Otherwise you're in for a very long road ahead."

He began to pace around the cell like a captured beast. "I done him in, alright? Five years back. Windham's brother. I wanted to teach him a lesson and things got out of hand, but I didn't mean it. Happy now?"

Ella celebrated on the inside but kept her demeanor calm. "Why didn't you just admit this at your trial?"

"Call me crazy but I didn't want to go to jail for the rest of my life." Steen sat back down and calmed himself. He'd just accidentally given himself a long custodial sentence.

"Agent Byford, I'm done here. Anything to add?"

"Not a thing. I think we've got everything we need. See you soon, Kevin."

The two agents left the suspect behind, still seething from his outburst. They made their way out of the holding cells and back up into the office.

Byford had been wrong, Ella thought. They didn't have everything they need.

There was still a very pressing matter to attend to.

They still needed to find out who the real killer was.

CHAPTER TWENTY FOUR

Tobias Campbell sat at a very old computer about ten yards from his glass prison cell, counting down the minutes, the seconds.

Every Wednesday, the Category A inmates of Maine Correctional Institute were given access to the prison library where they could use computers, read books, play games, or study. Tobias was the only prisoner in the facility listed higher than Category A (the mythical Category X that many prison officials denied even existing), meaning his routine was different from the others.

Tobias was prohibited from mixing with other prisoners, so guards wheeled a computer into his underground chamber every Wednesday evening. It was a formality more than anything, since Tobias didn't really use the computer, not that he had much time for technology anyway. The computer had no Internet access and even no access to the localized prison Intranet. It was just a barebones machine with basic games, pictures, and some music files. Tobias usually just sat there for an hour, looking at the screen while an armed guard kept watch.

But today, things were going to be a little different.

Tobias Campbell hadn't had a formal education, had never seen the inside of a school in his life. His entire upbringing took place within the carnival. A traveling carnival, with sideshow freaks, gaffs, conmen, and swindlers trying to make an easy buck off the gullible public. His father had been what was known as a carnival barker, the man whose job consisted of enticing people in to see their famous freak show. *There are only two kinds of freaks, ladies and gentlemen. Those created by God, and those made by man. The creature in this pit is a living breathing human being that once was... well, that's another story that happened a long time ago, a long way from here. Look if you must.*

Tobias's first job as a curious 10-year-old boy was to walk through the carnival grounds and locate the *marks,* punters who had money to burn and could therefore be milked dry. He'd slip past them, *marking* their back with a piece of blue chalk. That way, the carnies at the stalls would know they were the punters to keep on the edge of a victory. *Just one more try at ring toss. Come on, you'll definitely do it this time.*

138

He struggled to pull it off at first, always pushing a little too hard. When the person realized some kid had defaced their clothing, Tobias just pretended like he was a mischievous little runt and fled. But over time, he became an expert. He was like a ghost, watching customers from afar, chalking them and then dispersing into the crowds. From the age of 11 onwards, no one ever could catch him. His fingers were so nimble they were like clouds on the end of his palm.

But the real educators came from the carnival's performers. Clowns, illusionists, card sharks, pickpockets. The people that could not only manipulate objects in unique ways, but could bend a person's psychological responses to their advantage. Weaponized psychological manipulation. He recalled a magician making a coin disappear, over and over again, then explaining that it wasn't his hands doing the work, it was the power of distraction. The fingertips were just the bullet, he said, the rest of the body was the gun. *The closer you look, the less you see.*

The same man taught Tobias sleight of hand and how to apply it properly. He taught him how to guide a person's attention wherever you wanted it. Pattern recognition exploitation, he called it, fooling the brain into thinking something had occurred when it hadn't. Transferring a coin from one hand to the other, placing a ball in your pocket, swallowing a needle.

Or stealing something right in front of an armed guard.

Tobias's fingertips grazed the underside of the mouse while he scrolled up and down the page. It was an old type of mouse with the ball inside, ancient by even his standards. It was all he deserved, he apparently.

"Officer, I think I'm done here," Tobias said. "I really have no use for this machine. Plus, I'm not feeling very good."

"Still got three minutes," the guard said.

Tobias smiled, sat back in his chair and put his hands behind his head and coughed loudly. He watched the clock in the corner of the screen and counted down until the moment of glory.

Just three minutes, he thought.

Three minutes until he could see Agent Dark again.

***

Every cell in Maine Correctional Institute had a pull cord tied up at the rear. In the case of emergency, an inmate was to pull the cord for immediate medical assistance. The cords in Category A cells were placed cruelly high, and in a catastrophic medical emergency, the chances of an inmate being able to reach the cord were almost zero. It was one of the prison system's little tricks to kill off notable inmates, Tobias knew.

Tobias untied his cell-cord every day, so it dangled down at head height. Not that he'd ever used it.

But that changed today.

Every day at the carnival, Tobias would watch the magician perform his act from the side of the stage. Even after a thousand shows, his tricks fascinated the boy. There was one trick above all else that he would watch with unbridled focus and attention, the one trick of which the magician never revealed the secret.

He used to call the trick Alive and Undead. The magician would call up a spectator from the audience to hold his pulse. Then, the magician would place a plastic bag over his head and claim he was going to cut off the oxygen to his brain. The resulting effect would be a zombie-like state of such euphoric highs that he couldn't feel pain.

Sure enough, the spectator would soon discover that the magician's pulse had stopped beating – an impossible feat, surely. The magician would then walk on glass, pierce his skin with needles and hammer nails into his nose – all without flinching.

How could it be? It was an illusion like no other, and one that left a lasting impression on the young boy watching from the wings. The mystery consumed young Tobias day and night, to the point that he fully believed the magician's stage patter might be true. Maybe he really did kill and revive himself every night? Even after years of begging and pleading, the magician never revealed the secrets of this bizarre illusion.

Then one winter morning, the carnival owner discovered the magician dead in his trailer. Suffocated, apparently, like all those nights cutting off his oxygen supply finally caught up with him. More mysteriously, was that the magician's notebook had vanished too.

The magician and his unexplainable death taught Tobias more about himself than school ever could. And this was how 14-year-old Tobias finally learned the secret to this illusion, and if he was being honest, it was something of a disappointment.

All he needed was a ball. Any ball, no matter its size or shape or toughness. A sponge ball would do, or a tennis ball.

Or the ball from an old computer mouse.

Back in his cell, Tobias concealed the ball in his armpit and sat on his bed. He remembered watching the magician from the side of the stage perform the same rite thirty years ago, wondering whether or not he was witnessing some esoteric supernatural practice.

A minute later, Tobias's pulse stopped beating.

There was nothing supernatural about it. The fact that it was a simple biological response was much more fascinating to him.

Tobias pulled the cord then collapsed onto the floor in a heap. Between violent spasms, he coughed up blood all over his white jumpsuit.

He'd watched a thousand magic performances, night in and night out for over a decade.

It was time to put on a show of his own.

CHAPTER TWENTY FIVE

Ella, Byford, and Sheriff Hunter stood between their offices in the NDPD precinct.

"It's him," Byford said. "It has to be."

Sheriff Hunter scratched his stubble. He looked like he hadn't seen a bed in weeks, Ella thought.

"Same. That man has trouble written all over him. He's got something to hide."

Both turned to Ella, waiting for her input. She looked back towards the holding cell area then tied back her admittedly greasy hair. She simply shook her head. Byford and Hunter both sighed in unison.

"Ella, seriously? Just take one look at that man and you'll get everything you need to know."

"There are a few things that don't add up to me."

The sheriff's phone rang but he clicked it to voicemail. "That man is a career thief. He'd steal anything that isn't nailed down and then take the nails too."

"Exactly," Ella said. "Stealing is in his blood. Alan Yates was rich as hell. Loveridge was an antiques dealer. Windham had thousands of rare coins. Yet nothing was stolen from any of the scenes? You think a hardened thief like that isn't gonna sweep those places clean? Plus, he's only been free for a month. He needs the money, and these crime scenes gave him the perfect opportunity."

Neither Byford nor Hunter had a response.

"Secondly, why would he confess to one murder and not the others? He just cemented himself a long term, maybe even life inside. He might as well go the whole hog."

"Alright," Byford said, "anything else, or are you done crushing our spirits?"

"One more. What motivation does Steen have to kill these people anyway? It's not like they have dirt on him. He's dirtier than a pigsty and he openly admits it. If these victims *did* have something on Steen, wouldn't they have dished it while Steen was safe behind bars? They've had five freaking years."

"Valid points, but I still think it's him," Hunter said. "We've had a few cops go through his house while you were in there. He's got quite a few coins."

"But none from 1964, I'm guessing," Ella said. "Just like the one I found in his jacket."

"Well, no, but still lots of coins."

"The year is crucial. That's the key to this. If Steen was planning on killing, he would have a 1964 coin with him. The one I found wasn't."

Hunter threw his arms up in defiance. "Whatever you say. I need a beverage. I can't think straight right now."

"I'll join you," Byford said and followed Hunter down the corridor. Ella retreated into her office alone and collapsed on her seat. She planted her face down on the table, shut her eyes and drifted into the transcendent state between dream and reality, the state that nurtured subconscious connections between seemingly unrelated data.

Kevin Steen didn't fit. A career thief was a square peg, and the serial killer was a round hole. The two didn't go together no matter how hard you forced them. Their mindsets and philosophies were at odds with one another. The thief *took* from crime scenes, the serial killer *left* things behind. The thief stayed in the shadows, unobserved from start to finish. The serial killer made himself known, taunting, terrorizing, boasting of his handiwork. This unsub fell into the latter category. From what Ella could tell, Kevin Steen wasn't a show-off. If he *did* kill these three victims for whatever reason, he would done it as cleanly as possible and certainly wouldn't have left a calling card. If this was a follow-on from his murder from five years ago, wouldn't he have left coins in the victim's eyes back then too? And why would Steen so willingly wipe out the people he sold his so-called hot property to? All he was doing was sabotaging his own business.

What would Mia tell her to do here? The same thing she always did; strip away any preconceived notions and start with the basics. Ella brought up the patterns the unsub had shown.

He was targeting older men, between 58 and 62. Their ages and genders weren't a coincidence. This pattern would continue on with any future victims, of that Ella was certain.

At every scene, the number 1964 appeared. This number did not relate to the victims. It related to something else. It might be the killer's birth year, but the police database didn't show any suspects born that year with a criminal history who also had links to the coin collecting world.

Did the 1964 message need to be delivered in the form of coins, or were the coins surplus to requirement? Could he have spray-painted 1964 on the walls and delivered the same message? Could he have carved it into their skin?

No. The coins were vital. They couldn't be extracted from the profile.

She applied these patterns to historical serial cases and sieved through the information in her brain. Images, names, and dates flashed by in a blur, and she found herself looking at the mugshots of three obscure serial killers.

Luke Woodham, who left goat horns in his victims.

Michael Hardman, who left ripped Bibles at every scene.

Michael Kelly, who left behind strange masks.

These men had nothing in common with her unsub, she thought. The only similarity was that they left behind *something*. Ella broadened the parameters in her head came up with three more names.

Ted Bundy, who once left some of his girlfriend's clothing at a crime scene.

Dennis Rader, who left some his mother's underwear alongside a dead body.

And lastly and most clearly was her old friend Tobias Campbell, who'd scattered some of his mother's ashes at every scene.

Ella shot upright in her seat. It was these last three she zoned in on. In each case, the things left behind didn't belong to the killers. Bundy and Rader left theirs for a sexual thrill, while Campbell scattered his mother's ashes to frame his father.

The circumstances were different, but the idea was the same.

"Oh my God," she said, pounding her fist against the table. "Of course. Why didn't I think of that earlier?"

Ella leaped out of her chair and moved to the whiteboard. She scrawled some chaotic thoughts about her unsub, his victimology, and then applied the same framework to the historical cases running through her head.

There was a match.

She suddenly thought of her conversation with Aleister Black outside the precinct. He'd said that their killer had access to a 1964 coin collection.

He didn't say the collection had to necessarily belong to the killer.

Bundy's girlfriend's clothes were found at a crime scene, but she wasn't the killer. Rader's mother's clothes were found on a dead body, but she wasn't the killer either. These items were left behind as insults, signs of power and ownership. They were left on victims that were surrogates for their hatred.

It was no different here. This unsub is tying these murders to someone else, just like Bundy and Rader and Campbell did. This killer was a messenger, Ella thought. The object of his desire was someone around the ages of these men, someone born in 1964, someone who might not necessarily be connected to them.

"Byford," she shouted around the door, but couldn't see any sign of her partner or the sheriff. "Damn it."

This couldn't wait. She grabbed her jacket and headed back down towards the holding cells. There was someone in there who might just be able to help.

***

Ella ran back into the underground holding cells at the NDPD building. Kevin Steen was the only prisoner in the row. She ran up to his cage and grabbed the bars, suddenly reminding her of her visits to Maine Correctional Institute.

"Kevin," she shouted.

The suspect was lying on his wooden bed staring at the ceiling.

"Fuck off."

"Listen to me. I need your help, and if you help me, I can help you."

Steen rose to a sitting position. "Help you, huh?"

"Yes. What have you got to lose?"

Steen rubbed his hands together. "Alright, lady. Try me."

"You said you know every collector in this city, correct? Stolen from them, supplied to them, whatever."

Steen shrugged, but the look on his face was one of approval. "Maybe."

"Coins from 1964. Specialist coins. Do you recall anyone who collected those?"

White teeth showed through his wry smile. "What's it worth?"

"I don't know the values. Any value."

"Not the coins, doofus. The information."

Ella gripped the bars harder. "You know someone?" She had to break this man down, no matter what it took.

"I'll ask again – what's it worth?"

"A reduced sentence. Better prison conditions. You'll be treated like royalty inside."

"Absolute minimal sentence. Four years."

145

"Kevin, I can't promise…"

"Then get out of here," he interrupted.

"Okay, okay. I'll make sure that happens. Now please, lives are at stake."

Steen inspected his fingernails then bit a chunk out of one. "Yeah, I know a '64 collector. I ain't got his name though, and I never even met the man in the flesh."

Ella fell back from the bars and despaired. She wasn't here to play this man's games. "You don't have his name?"

"No, and it doesn't matter anyway, because you're not gonna find this guy in a million years."

"I can find anyone," Ella said.

"Grab a shovel and start digging six feet under then, because this guy died a few weeks back."

That doesn't change anything, she thought. *That just makes all the more sense.* "Who was he? What business did you do together?"

"Any '64 coins I came across, I kept them for him. Simple as that. Them coins were actually worth a dime or two. It was a big year for coin collectors because of the Olympics in Japan. The guy paid me to hold them."

Ella rattled her hand between the prison bars. She was getting impatient. "But how, if you never met him?"

"Very secretive man. Violent as hell. Complete lunatic, if you ask me."

"Answer the question," she demanded.

"He sent a messenger. This timid little kid. Shy as a schoolgirl, looked like one too. Me and some of the other boys used to give the kid a hard time. That kid must have grown up to really hate…," Steen froze mid-sentence as he finished the thought silently. "Oh… shit." The look on his face was a level of concern Ella hadn't seen from the man: rare emotion.

Ella remembered the moments she saw Daniel Garcia, Aleister Black, and Kevin Steen for the first time. With all of them, there was a niggling doubt that she might be wrong or might have misinterpreted the facts that seemed so clear.

But this time, there was no doubt, just pure certainty. She'd bet absolutely everything she owned.

"Where do I find this kid? How do I contact him?"

Steen"s eyes glazed as over as he lost himself deep in thought. Three deep breaths later, he said:

"You bring me my phone and you let me do the talking."

CHAPTER TWENTY SIX

Just like the other three, the man made the journey to his next destination on foot. He walked past an Italian restaurant that was just closing its doors for the evening. A grocery store owner switched off the lights and pulled down the shutters to his establishment. A seedy bar pushed its customers out onto the midnight streets, some who still had beers in their hands.

He crossed the road to avoid any large groups and kept his head down. Hood pulled up, but only enough to suggest it was a respite from the cold. His destination loomed in the distance, and as he passed the old cinema, he turned left down the narrow path leading to the rear of the buildings on this row. He slid himself into a tight alleyway that backed onto a towering wall, away from prying eyes. All the shops were shut at this time of night too, so he was as isolated as it came. Once he was behind his destination, he sat down beside a pile of trash bags that he used for both protection and warmth. If any eager lovers used the place for intimacy over the next hour or two, which he'd seen happen, he could just plead homelessness.

Sitting here now, waiting for the right hour, reminded of him why he was doing all this. The sense of discomfort he felt sitting on this damp floor with barely enough space to stretch brought back familiar memories, familiar distress. The times he'd been locked under the stairs while his dad drowned out his cries with music. The lies he told to his teachers, about how those cuts on his cheek were just cat scratches. Any time he felt that surge of pain, recollections of his lost innocence invaded every sense. He thought it would disappear with time, but every year it seemed to get worse. Now, at 24 years old, he couldn't even prick his finger without it reminding him of some abusive episode or cruel directive from his youth.

There was one remedy, and that was to kill the author of his pain.

But fate had intervened. Two weeks ago, his father had fallen asleep and stayed there. He never woke up and never would, and that simple act ensured the boy would never get the redemption he needed. All those times he fantasized about slitting the old man's throat in the middle of night would have to remain fantasies forever.

Unless he could track down the men who reminded him of his father. His precious coin collecting buddies, his dealers, the old men he bargained with for these little pieces of junk. He remembered the times his dad would wake him up at five am, drag him around flea markets and garage sales until his feet scorched with blisters. Sifting through endless sacks of coins in trash cans behind banks until his fingers bled. The rare times he found a worthwhile coin, his dad took it from him and gave no thanks. The times he found nothing, he got a beating for his efforts.

Always looking for that one piece of treasure that would change everything. His dad said it was out there somewhere: one little coin that could provide the fortune he craved so badly. They never found it. All of the coins he found were worthless, maybe fifty dollars maximum per coin.

He checked his phone. 00:34. His father had passed at one am, so it was only fitting that the others died at the same time too. If he recreated the circumstances of his father's last moments down to a tee, there was a chance it would feel like the real thing. The others had given him a feeling of control he'd never felt in his life, and maybe with enough of that, he could finally put an end to his crippling trauma.

00:37 now. By the time he'd broken in, it would be the hour of reckoning. He climbed to his feet, edged around to the back door and plunged his knife between the door and door frame. At that moment, his cellphone began to vibrate.

Cursing the distraction, he reached in and pulled out a flashing device.

KEVIN STEEN CALLING.

Wow, the rat bastard finally escaped from jail. How about that? Perfect. He'd make a good number five. He ignored the call, focusing on the task at hand.

But the old thief was relentless. His phone vibrated non-stop, call after call, crushing the man's concentration levels. When he looked at his screen again, he saw a message.

CALL ME IMMEDIATELY. THEY ARE ON TO YOU.

Curiosity and fear double-up inside of him. Who? Who was on to him? How could anyone know? He'd been meticulous in his planning, precise in his execution. No one could know about him, least of all Kevin Steen.

KEVIN STEEN CALLING, this time for the sixth time in two minutes. He let go of his knife, clicked the answer button, and spoke in a whisper.

"Hello?"

"Hey, is that L's son? Do I have the right number?"

Kevin's gravelly voice, as unmistakable as ever. "Yes. Kevin, what's wrong?"

"Are you at home right now?"

"No. I'm out."

"Where at?"

"None of your business."

"Alright. Look, I just wanted to say I'm sorry to hear about your old man. I have something for you. Where can I meet you to hand it over?"

Something didn't seem right about this. Kevin Steen was a scumbag of the highest order, and here he was being friendly? "Kevin, you said they're onto me. Who's onto me?"

"You never heard of a rib, buddy? It's just a little trick to get you to pick up the damn phone."

"You're an asshole. I'm going."

"Wait up. You in town? You want to get a…"

The line went dead.

Something was going on. That call was suspicious. It was too specific. Why did he call right now, of all times?

He had to get this over with quickly. He picked up his knife and jammed it back into the door frame.

***

Ella was out of the holding cells, out of the precinct and into her car. The phone call between Jimmy and this nameless suspect had lasted less than a minute, but it was enough to get a rough estimate of where the caller might be located. Right now, all she knew was that it was within a five-mile radius of the city center, and that was where she was headed. Back at the precinct, a member of the tech team was triangulating it down to a more specific area, but it would take time.

The midnight streets had little life in them, but just enough to make Ella stop and stare whenever she passed a moving body. Kevin had given her a description of the man she was looking for, but Steen hadn't seen him in five years so his accuracy could be off the mark. Regardless, she stopped and weighed up everyone she passed by: the

149

lone figure at the ATM machine, the midnight drifter on the search for late night entertainment.

At the traffic lights, she grabbed her phone and dialed Byford for the third time. Again, it went to voicemail. Was he mad at her for not jumping to conclusions about Steen? She understood his frustrations better than anyone, but to be upset with someone for not immediately assuming guilt was alien to her. Innocent until proven guilty was still a fundamental principle of the legal system. She guessed Byford just wanted to get home, just like she did, but not before she'd gotten to the bottom of this.

"Nigel, call me when you get this. I know who our unsub is and I'm in town trying to find him."

She hung up, clutched her phone in her hand as she navigated the wheel. A second later, a number flashed up her screen. She didn't recognize it.

"Hello?" She switched it to speaker.

"Agent Dark, it's Jessica," the voice said. Jessica was the member of the tech team triangulating the cell's position.

"Jessica, what have you found?"

"I couldn't get an exact reading. The signal bounced between three telephone poles in the zone, all across a two-mile radius. West Avenue, Bayard Street and Nowland Lane."

Ella slammed the brakes on and mounted the curb. The names didn't mean anything to her. "Damn it, so he could be anywhere within two miles? That's a lot of ground to cover."

"No, not quite. It means the call came from somewhere in the middle of them. I've emailed you a diagram of the locations."

"Thank you." Ella hung up and found the email. A picture was attached inside. She opened it up to find a map of the immediate area, and three red dots indicating the cell tower locations.

How was she supposed to find him here? She zoomed in on street names, buildings, shops, not recognizing any that sprung up. What was her best hope? Call for backup, search the entire area? Every single street, building and back alleyway? Was it doable, or would it just be a waste of time? Hell, it had been nearly ten minutes since Steen made the call, so the suspect could have long fled the area by now.

She scoured the map again, feeling helplessness beginning to mount. Her suspect had been here, walked the same paths and breathed the same air. The only thing keeping them from meeting was her abilities. She zoomed in on the building names, hunting for anything that might have a link to this unsub.

The names all blurred into one to the point they meant nothing. Nothing stood out. Nothing captured her attention. Then she scanned her surroundings one last time and tried to put herself in the unsub's head. Would Steen's call have spooked him or would he carry on with his intentions regardless? As she pieced things together, she noticed she was staring a jewelry store nestled between two vape shops.

WE BUY GOLD, the sign said.

A surge of electricity traveled down her neck, into her spine. She jerked upright in her seat.

Something called out to her. A faraway thought that offered some kind of answer, if only she could clarify it among the accumulating thoughts.

Where'd she heard that before?

The day before. She'd seen it outside the pawn shop. She suddenly recalled her conversation with the owner who'd given her the lead on Aleister Black.

As she replayed the conversation in her head, she felt the doubts again, like it was all unrelated. Then she remembered something Ace had said before they parted ways.

I only sold to one coin collector and the old bastard died weeks ago. Heart attack, I think.

"Oh shit. You gotta be kidding me," she called as she pulled up the map. That was it. That was the answer to all this. She pulled up the JPEG picture again and frantically zoomed across as she hunted for the street she needed.

Dragon Run Road.

Five streets away.

She texted Byford the address. Did he even have his phone with him? Had he gone back to the motel already?

The engine roared to life. She sped off into the night, not waiting for anyone or anything.

Time to finish this.

CHAPTER TWENTY SEVEN

Ella dumped her car outside Aces & Eights and jumped out. She yanked the old store's wooden door to the point it nearly fell off its hinges.

Locked as expected.

She stepped back into the road and analyzed the building layout. The whole row of buildings here were connected, so there were no side entrances or fire doors that she could see. She took off towards the end of the row, passing an adjoining gaming store, vet, and Thai restaurant. That's when she saw the narrow entranceway leading to the rear of the row. She slipped down in haste, coming to a large yard that doubled as the disposal area for each establishment. Trash bags and discarded boxes lay in no particular arrangement, finding the waste from the restaurant took up most of the floorspace.

Ella moved to the section she believed would belong to Aces & Eights based on geographical guesswork and, upon seeing the dislodged fire door, knew she was in the right place.

Just like the basement door in Barry Windham's garden, there were scuff marks on the wooden door frame. Ella turned the knob and the door fell open.

She drew her pistol, flashlight, and hurried inside. Her flashlight illuminated a rack of bikes, some old guitars, video game consoles, a glass case of jewelry. She was on the ground floor, back where she was a day ago.

Her breath came in hot, painful waves. There were two options the next few minutes would bring; either she'd find Ace's dead body in a pool of blood or she'd come face to face with a psychopathic serial killer. She'd called for backup, but it could be ten or more minutes away. This was a venture she had to make alone.

Ella sidestepped through the store, keeping her movements silent. Her flashlight danced in orange circles across the walls, the floors, and the store counter. The only exit other than the front door was the storeroom, which Ella accessed by climbing over the counter area. She found the wooden door half-open, then by her flashlight, saw a staircase leading to the upstairs of the house. Ace had said he lived here. That must be his living quarters.

Ella pushed forward, taking each step gently, keeping her weight above her knees. One or two steps creaked loudly, suggesting intrusion to someone familiar with the store's characteristics. The staircase spiraled around to a landing area not unlike any modest home. There was one door to her left, one to her right and one straight ahead. All were ajar, giving no declarations of recent entry.

She stopped and listened to the air, hearing nothing but the sound of her thumping heart.

If this man was in here, what could she say to him that might make him yield? She knew his mindset, but nothing about him that she could exploit to bring him down. He was a mission-oriented killer, hell-bent on vengeance for some perceived wrongdoing. Unsubs like him were the most dangerous of all. They'd already abandoned reality in favor of their murderous fantasy worlds, and therefore had no real awareness of consequences. Threatening death or imprisonment did nothing to deter them from carrying out their homicidal operations. To them, it was the most important thing in the world, the only thing that mattered.

Her only hope was that she could take him down before any lives were lost.

Ella snuck to the first door, threw it open and looked inside. It was a stock room of items: electronics, speakers, TVs, outdated technologies. Not here. She crept to the room opposite, drowning in adrenaline when she saw the outline of a giant figure in the darkness. The beast occupied the entire corner of the room, his head almost reaching the ceiling. Her flashlight lit up the figure's creamy skin, inhuman expression and perfectly smooth genitals.

A mannequin. Ella had to stop herself cursing out loud. For a moment, she feared she was dealing with someone of inhuman proportions. She checked the rest of the room, finding a toilet, bath, and sink. More boxes of junk took up the spaces between them.

By her math, the next room had to be Ace's bedroom.

Ella kept herself calm, composed, and focused. She gripped her pistol, finding solace in its touch. This unsub didn't use guns as far as she knew, so the advantage was hers. But an unaware victim had no such protection.

Ella's thoughts scrambled as an earsplitting scream pierced the air. The lack of visibility in the corridor heightened her other senses, and the sheer volume of the cry caused intense physical pain. In a split second, her calm composure all but vanished. Her fight response took over as her primary drive. She was into the last door less than a blink later, shouldering it open with brute force.

She saw it by yellow lamplight. Two figures, both locked in a deathly embrace. It took Ella a moment to make sense of the scene in front of her.

Ace, the large, bearded store owner, was at the mercy of another man. Up against the wall, his attacker stood behind him with a knife to his throat. Ace, red-eyed and wearing nothing but shorts, had the face of a man who believed death was imminent. His tiny eyes were widened with abject terror.

"Stop! FBI!" Ella shouted.

The man was much younger than she'd anticipated. Early twenties? His gingery blonde hair reminded her of someone she'd seen recently. She connected the pieces together, realizing now she'd seen the man only this morning.

Only he wasn't a man when she saw him. He was a child. He was the boy in the newspaper article from 2002.

The attacker renewed his grip on the hostage. "Who are you? Why are you here?" he screamed. His voice was soft, nasally, feminine. She remembered Kevin Steen saying he reminded him of a schoolgirl.

"What's your name?" Ella asked.

"I don't have one. Now get back before I cut this guy's throat to shreds."

Ace reached up to alleviate the pressure on his neck, but his attacker pushed him off.

"Sir, please listen to me. Your dad is gone and isn't coming back. Taking revenge on his friends isn't going to help you."

"What the hell do you know? You think you know me?"

Ella had to keep this man calm. She saw how he reacted at the Barry Windham crime scene. Rage meant violence.

"No, I don't know much about you at all, but I know why you're doing this, and I'm here to tell you that you don't have to. I can help you."

"You're lying. You don't know anything about me."

Ella saw a crack she could open up. If she couldn't talk this man down, and she doubted she could, she needed time to get a clean shot. If she could just get Ace out of the way for a split second, she could take this man down.

"No I don't, so why don't you tell me? Why have you killed three people? Alan, Jimmy, Barry. Why?"

154

"Don't say their names. Those pieces of shit don't deserve to be spoken of ever again."

Ella kept it going. Time was her friend here. "Why? What did they do to you?"

"They made my life hell is what they did. My dad's coin collecting buddies. Death is too good for them."

"I'm confused here. What exactly do you despise about coin collecting?"

"I couldn't give a shit about coin collecting. My dad was the collector, but he dragged me into it. Every day, he'd make me rummage through trash, go to stupid garage sales, spend my entire life looking for coins. It ruined me. It broke me."

They said the greatest burden a child could bear was the unlived life of his parents. Here was living proof. "But why Alan and Jimmy and Barry? They did nothing to you."

"They knew my old man. I was dragged to see them every single week, sitting alone in their houses while my dad talked shit with them for hours. If I complained or made a sound, my dad would smack the hell out of me. These assholes overlooked that." He pushed his knife harder into Ace's neck. "Didn't you?"

"Brad, we had no idea. I swear on my life," Ace shouted. "We thought your father was a good man."

Ella caught his name.

"Bullshit. You knew full well what he was like. You just didn't care because he gave you money. That was all you cared about. All my dad cared about. All he wanted was one coin to make him rich. I thought that maybe, just maybe, if I found a coin that was worth a dime, he might start loving me. Never happened."

"I'm sorry, Brad," cried Ace. "I didn't know. You don't have to do this."

"Brad, I know all about childhood trauma. Killing these men won't make that pain go away. You have an internal pain that you're trying to address externally. Why don't you talk about it with me?"

"You think I'm a sucker? The second I let this guy go, you're going to shoot me. Well, that isn't gonna happen."

Ella's finger itched on the trigger. Brad was clearly in control of his mental faculties, not psychotic. He knew what he was doing. What was the solution here? Wait until Brad killed Ace and then fire? Or take a shot right now and hope for the best?

No, another good man couldn't die because of this psychopath. There had to be a way to make him lower his guard. All she needed was a fleeting moment.

"Brad, those coins you left at the crime scenes. They were your father's?"

"Yeah."

"I'm not sure if you know this, but your father wasn't exactly a very knowledgeable collector," Ella said. She wasn't sure where she was going with this, but it would come to her. Backup couldn't be too far away now. But even when they arrived, Ace's life would still hang in the balance.

So it was on her to draw this man out.

"One of those coins you had. It was worth *a lot*."

"What? Stop lying to me. Does anyone tell the truth anymore?" Brad screamed. Ella saw the anger and frustration beginning to mount. She didn't have long before he reached his limit.

"I'm not. We had them all appraised by an expert. Six coins in total, right? Five of them were common, but that one... holy moly."

"You're talking out of your ass. Which one?"

Kennedy, Japan, China was how she remembered them. "The Chinese one. Shen-si Province, 1964."

"That coin isn't worth a thing."

"You're right, it's not. Not usually. But the coin you had was a misprint. They'd etched one of the characters wrong."

Brad held her stare with his black beady eyes. It was difficult to gauge his response by the light of the single lamp in the room, but what she did see was his grip slightly loosen.

"Lies," he said.

"Don't believe me? I can show you the proof right here."

The atmosphere in the room changed. Ella felt Brad's intentions altering.

"Prove it."

Ella reached into her pocket, wondering where exactly to go from here. If she didn't produce something, Brad would act out in frustration. She found something plastic inside her jacket.

The coin I found on Steen, she thought.

It wasn't the Chinese coin, but under the shadow of darkness, she hoped Brad wouldn't see that.

"Here," she pulled out the item. "Here it is. They actually gifted it to me since I was the one who found it."

"How much?" Brad asked with a staccato voice.

"A hundred grand, give or take. Maybe even more to a collector in Asia."

"Give it to me," Brad said.

Ella put the coin back in her pocket, away from closer inspection. "I was actually going to give it to Ace. He's got eight kids. He needs it more than me."

"No, you give it to me. It's mine. I found it," Brad shouted.

Ella let the moment hang in the air. "Alright, but you gotta come and get it."

"Throw your gun down. Over there," Brad pointed to the far corner of the room.

Ella debated it. Was that a good idea? Did she have any other option?

She applied the safety latch and threw the pistol twenty feet away.

"Happy?"

Brad lowered his knife and took two steps to the left. "Show me the coin again."

Ella shook her head. "Not until you get away from Ace. Then I'll help you." She watched Brad's micro-expressions change as he weighed up the situation in his head. Curiosity turned to trepidation, and then finally, vulnerability. He tensed his shoulders, raised his knife, and pointed it at Ella.

"Coin. Now."

Beyond the walls, Ella heard the sound of approaching police sirens.

Brad heard them too.

No, not now. I'm so close.

"You bitch. You don't want to help me at all. You just want to take me down."

"Brad, wait..." she pleaded, but it was too late. He turned, thrashed his knife around and caught Ace with the tip. Ace toppled backwards, clutching his shoulder as the attacker turned his rage towards Ella.

The last thing she saw was the gleaming tip of a steel blade heading right between her eyes.

Ella felt the hardwood floor against her spine. She'd avoided the blow but had tied up with her attacker and fallen to the ground. The blow had disoriented her for what felt like an eternity, but in reality, it was barely two seconds.

The boy had been quick, quicker than she anticipated. He was reasonably built, and he had speed and agility on his side too. Brad's cries of rage combined with Ace's screeching moans created a symphony of hellish sounds in her ear canals.

She jerked fast to avoid the boy's strikes, coming at her in forceful but inaccurate blows. The knife pierced the wooden floorboards with every thrust, so loud it sounded as though it was her own eardrums being punctured. Ella arched up her knees and booted him in the abdomen, feeling his brittle bones crack at her feet. He flew off her, crashing against the far wall but resuming his attacks without stopping for breath. She caught sight of Ace, collapsed on the sofa with a bleeding wound in his arm.

Brad came at her relentlessly, swinging his blade like a hooligan with a baseball bat. Ella sidestepped the oncoming attacks then found she was backing herself into a corner. Her priority was to get the weapon out of his hands to make it a fair fight. She fell back into the darkened corner of the room, dropped to a crouching position and charged at Brad's mid-section.

The tip of his knife tinged her back for a brief moment. Ella cursed her misplaced ambition because a knife in the spine meant instant paralysis. She maneuvered around to his back, clutched his wrist from behind and shook violently to dislodge the weapon, but Brad pushed his feet against the wall, sending him and Ella flying back down the ground. The impact on the solid floor winded her, with Brad's weighty torso crushing her ribs at the same time. She coughed up a spout of blood, knowing there'd be some internal organ damage somewhere. She didn't have time to worry about it.

Still holding his wrist and keeping it immobile, Ella clutched her attacker around the neck with her forearm and choked with every ounce of power left in her. She felt his neck muscles expand and contract like a balloon, until phlegm poured from his mouth and nostrils. The boy was fading, and she wouldn't let go until he was out. She tightened her grip, but a second later, all of her energy depleted with a single blow. The pain burned down her forearm and into her elbow with brutal intensity. Blood poured, dousing them both.

Then she saw the knife digging into her flesh. In desperation, Brad had somehow twisted his wrist and searched for the nearest attack point he could. Brad shot free from Ella's grip, climbed on top of her. She defended his blows and grabbed his forearms, but the distance between the knife edge and her throat wasn't great enough.

Footsteps thundered somewhere below them. A voice shouted something, but Ella couldn't discern who it was or what they said. She was too busy trying to survive. The noise provided a momentary distraction and Ella was able to scramble up from her position, but Brad grabbed her from behind, wrapped his legs around her pushed the knife edge against her throat one more time. She held it back with both hands, but her energy levels were depleting rapidly. The pain was constant, sharp, and reaching unbearable levels.

Bang.

A figure manifested at the door, gun in hand.

"Stop right there. Let her go. Now," Byford shouted.

"No!" Brad screamed at the new arrival. "Someone is dying tonight."

"No one has to die tonight, my friend. Get up, or I'll make this hurt."

"Shoot him," shouted Ella. "I can't hold on."

"No target," Byford replied.

"Don't care. Do it."

It was a risk that had to be taken. Rather she be killed by an honest bullet than the hands of a serial killer.

"Just hold on, Ella. Trust me."

"Shoot. Please. I can't…"

Some people said your life flashed before your eyes the moment you died, but the truth was it didn't. You just froze and pulled a revolting face because you were too scared to think.

Bang.

A deafening sound echoed around the room, like condensed thunder packed into a tiny space. Ella squeezed her eyes shut, felt the vibrations run through her, and prayed that something would be on the other side.

Bang.

Again.

"Ella, get up!" Byford screamed. When she came unstuck, there was no smoking pistol in her partner's hands, but a hyperventilating man was standing behind her with a plank of wood in his hands. He fell back with exhaustion, and Ella realized that Ace had just smashed the life out of her aggressor with his last ounce of strength.

Here was her chance. Brad was still only disoriented because she could feel resistance when she pushed his blade away. She scrambled to her feet, Brad in tow. She clutched his arm, pulled him closer to her and smashed her palm against his nose. His bones shattered beneath the force, painting her hand a deep shade of red. Brad flailed his blade around, lightly caressing Ella's skin, and then she saw an opportunity for victory. She ran at the boy, coming at him from the right-hand side. She wrapped her left leg around his stomach and brought him down to the ground face-first. Brad screamed out, kicking like a maniac, but Ella had full control over his lower half. She clutched his ankle, hyper-extending to the point of snapping it in two.

Brad screamed into the floor, trying to reach behind him and stab, but the position made it impossible. She kept the ankle lock in place while Byford ran in and pushed his foot against Brad's wrists. She pulled the submission harder, and it was clear that both Brad's energy and willpower were fading away.

His hand outstretched, dropping his weapon.

"Go," Ella shouted.

Byford cuffed the boy's hands. Then his feet.

Ella collapsed against the wall, catching her breath. She studied the wound on her arm, knowing it would get worse before it got better. She crawled over to Ace, wounded but still breathing. Brothers in battle, she thought.

"Ace, are you okay? We'll get medics here in a second."

"Been better, been worse," he said with a smile.

"You saved my ass," Ella said. "Big time."

Ace denied it. "No, your partner saved your ass. He distracted the kid, I just smacked him. Team effort."

"My coin," Brad said as he rolled onto his back. "You have to give it to me."

Ella looked at Ace, telling him the truth with a simple glance.

"Brad," Ace said. "That coin isn't worth shit. You got played."

Brad went to make a sound, but Byford stood over him with his pistol trained on him. The killer fell quiet.

"Game over," Byford said.

CHAPTER TWENTY EIGHT

Ella Dark and Nigel Byford packed up their equipment and readied themselves to leave Delaware. Sheriff Hunter walked into the room, a little less tired than he looked before. He must have gotten some sleep the night before, Ella thought.

"I'm sad you're leaving us," the sheriff said. "Mighty fine work on both your parts."

"Don't thank me. Ella's the one who figured it out," Byford said.

Ella appreciated the admiration, but it always came with embarrassment. "Thanks, guys. I'm sorry to be leaving too."

Sheriff Hunter put his hands on his hips. "Sorry for doubting you. I feel an awesome fool."

Ella stuffed her laptop, cables, and paperwork into her bag and zipped it up. The thrill of the chase was why she agreed to these jobs, but the feeling of packing up following a successful case was unbeatable.

If only there weren't just as many problems awaiting her when she got back.

"Don't mention it. I made enough mistakes myself. I got through three suspects before I found the right one," she laughed.

"Not a bad average, all things considered," said Sheriff Hunter. "Anyway, our killer is singing like a bird. Looks like he's been waiting a long time to wax lyrical about his plans."

"What's he saying?" Ella asked.

"Well, his name's Brad Callis, 24 years old. His old man, Donald Callis, was pretty strict on him as a kid. Used to beat him black and blue. He was planning on killing his old man, but he woke up dead a couple of weeks ago. Heart attack. It sent the kid down a spiral."

"Of course," Ella said. "His father died in his sleep. That's why he had to kill these men in their sleep. That's why he flew into a rage when Barry Windham woke up."

Sheriff Hunter pointed at Ella. "Good thinking. All our victims were friends of his dad's too. Part of the same coin collecting circles."

Ella thought about the three lost lives, and now one more young life that would never see the outside of a prison cell again. Brad Callis was never given a chance, so he took away other people's chances in a futile attempt at redemption. He had tried to erase his past through violence and instead ended up erasing his future. A tale as old as time, Ella thought.

"Meet me downstairs when you're done. I'll drive you to the airport," Sheriff Hunter said. He saw himself out.

Byford unplugged the last of his cables, put it in his satchel and threw the strap over his shoulder. "Looks like there's no doubt about it," he said. "You've caught a killer."

"*We've* caught a killer," she corrected. "If you'd have been a second later, I might not be here right now."

"What else are partners for?" Byford asked. "Some great moves you had back there. I've never seen a cop put someone in an ankle lock before."

"Oh yeah," Ella laughed, "that's my secret weapon."

Byford opened the door and held it for his partner. "Look, I'll be honest, before I got here, I was worried."

Ella shouldered her bag, checked the room for anything she'd missed. "You were?"

"Yeah. I'd never been partnered with a rookie before, and I didn't really like the idea of it. But you've taught me a few things. If you want my honest opinion, Mia Ripley is a fool for letting you go."

There came the embarrassment again. Ella felt her cheeks flush red. "I appreciate it, partner. I was hesitant too, and I judged you a little bit, but you proved me wrong. I can't wait to get on the next case with you. If you'd be willing, of course."

Byford held his hand out for a high five. Ella took it.

"Without a doubt. But hopefully we'll get some rest before that day. Let's get out of here."

Ella shut the door behind them and headed out of the precinct with her new partner. Home was only a few hours away, and she couldn't help but think of the trials and tribulations that awaited her. Mark, her father's mystery, Tobias's notes. Suddenly, this successful murder investigation felt like a minor victory.

CHAPTER TWENTY NINE

Tobias Campbell lay on a stretcher outside McLean Hospital in Maine, around two miles from the prison grounds. After collapsing to the floor of his cell and coughing up blood, concerned officers ordered immediate medical assistance. McLean Hospital was the prison's dedicated medical facility.

Campbell had spent the past thirty-seven minutes spluttering, convulsing, and rolling his pupils into the back of his head. Only the whites of his eyes were visible, like he was some kind of hellish demon.

The whole time, he'd manipulated his pulse to give the impression his internal organs were failing him.

"About time this happened," one of the guards said.

"Tell me about it," the other replied.

Two nurses wheeled Campbell up the ramp, through the hospital doors and into an elevator. One nurse stayed behind. In a few minutes, Campbell would be taken to a secure hospital room of which escape was impossible.

He couldn't let things get that far.

One nurse. Two guards. Three total.

He squeezed the ball in his armpit, cutting off the blood supply to his pulse. The monitor around his arm began to beep. All eyes in the elevator turned to the dying man.

One nurse grabbed the monitor and checked the data. "He's fading," she shouted. "He needs midazolam."

"He's on his way out," the guard said.

"Leave him be," the other laughed.

Tobias felt the moment in his bones. His vision was impaired due to his method acting, but he could always sense the right moment to strike. Another trick from the magician. You just *felt* the best moment to misdirect the participant.

As the sedative came down, Tobias's predatory instincts returned. It was a sensation he hadn't felt for fifteen years, but it was like they never left. He rose from the cusp of death, grabbing the woman's hand

and jumping from his stretcher bed in the same movement. The woman didn't have time to move or think. Tobias used her needle as his weapon, driving it into the neck of the uninterested guard on one side of the elevator. Tobias pushed the syringe down himself, emptying the extreme sedative into the man's bloodstream. With the other hand, he picked out the guard's electric taser.

"Fuck!" the other guard screamed, reaching for his pistol. Tobias moved like a predator, crossing the elevator in the blink of an eye. Before the guard even had his pistol pointed at him, Tobias had the taser buried into the guard's stomach, launching him into rapid shock. The nurse cowered into the corner, hand over her mouth. She frantically pushed buttons on the elevator control panel.

"Stop the elevator and I'll let you live," Tobias said calmly. He walked towards her, taser aimed at her stomach. "Three, two…"

The nurse pushed the *HOLD* button and the elevator stayed in place.

The gullibility of man, he thought. "Make a sound and I'll kill you," Tobias said. "Get over there, in the corner."

The nurse obliged, cowering in fear. Covering her head, like it would somehow keep the man at bay.

Tobias went back to the first guard, limp on the ground, but still breathing. Tobias locked his arm around his neck, twisted, and snapped the bones like frail twigs.

He'd already predicted the nurse's reaction at the sight of murder. "Shhh," he said before her screams emerged. "Behave and you'll get out of here alive."

The second guard sat crumpled in the corner, powerless and vulnerable. Tobias approached him and assumed the same position.

"Toby, please don't. I'll…" the guard breathed.

Snap. Neck bones shattered in two. It had been a long time since Tobias took a life, least of all two in one sitting, and he'd all but forgotten just how good it was. That feeling of playing God, the lord of life and death.

"And then there were two," he said to the nurse.

"You're… not ill?" she cried. "But how did you…"

He slowly approached the cowering woman and cornered her. Killing someone was one thing but instilling a sense of oncoming death in someone was unlike anything else in the world. In that moment, you were bigger than God. You controlled destiny.

Tobias buzzed the taser.

"Please. You said you'd let me live."

"I say a lot of things." He dug the taser into the nurse's neck and relished the physical breakdown that followed. She went into a fit of seizures and crumpled on the ground. With no one around, he took his time.

Tobias savored the aroma of death. It was like an old friend had finally come to visit again. He pushed the button for the top floor of the hospital. The hard part was over. The fact that no alarms were sounding meant his people had done their jobs correctly. This was the culmination of a long, complex plan.

At his destination, he walked out, leaving behind an elevator mass grave in his wake. The fire exit door was already lodged open for him. A few seconds later, he was out in the cool night air, with nothing but a staircase between him and freedom. He felt no need to rush. This moment had been a long time coming. The slower he walked, the bigger the insult to the prisons, the politicians, and the FBI directors who thought they could keep him locked in a cage for the rest of his life.

The world was his again. Alive and undead.

CHAPTER THIRTY

After a delayed flight, Ella Dark finally got back to D.C. in the early evening. She picked up her car at the airport and, instead of heading back home, detoured to the FBI offices. Before she'd left for Delaware, she'd run her dad's mysterious receipt through the graphology software at the HQ, and by now she should have had the results back.

There was also the matter of her relationship that she didn't want to address yet. She had enough trauma to worry about, and she still felt woozy from her arm wound. She wasn't in the right headspace to break up with an abuser just yet. As far as Mark knew, she was still in Delaware. It would stay that way until tomorrow.

Ella made her way to her desk in the Intelligence Division. A couple of late-night workers were still around, a few of which seemed happy to see Ella back in her old haunt. She set up her laptop and opened the graphology program she had installed.

TIME ELAPSED: 51 HOURS
DOCUMENTS CHECKED: 3,215,497,411
RESULTS: 17
95% MATCH: 4

"Wow," she said. She never expected to get a match, let alone four of them. Ninety-five percent match results were considered to be so accurately matched that they could be entered as evidence in a court of law.

She checked the four documents. The first was a form for planning permission written in 1998. Back when forms were done by hand, Ella thought. The permission had been requested by a man named Owen William Angels for his new business.

"Oh my God," she said. She remembered the initials on her father's receipt. OWA.

This must be the man.

She looked at the rest of the forms. The next was a tax relief bill from 2001 in the same handwriting. Next was a letter of appeals to the local government.

The last one was where her dread peaked.

166

According to the document on her screen, this Owen William Angels man had been arrested on suspicion of murder in 2003. He'd signed the document by hand with the same *OWA* Ella saw on her dad's receipt.

Who was this man, and why was her father acquainted with him?

She dug a little deeper and searched the FBI database for the name. His information popped up immediately.

Name: Owen William Angels.

Born: 05-31-1970

Occupation: Unknown

Address: Unknown

Prior Offences: 13

She went back to the documents and found that the tax relief bill was for Angels's company: Red Diamond.

"Oh Christ," she said. Red Diamond was a very well-known, very underground operation that operated in Virginia when she was a kid. Everyone in her old town had a story about the group, some people even claimed to have a brush with the members themselves. Whenever someone passed away in Staunton, Virginia, someone would start a rumor that the Diamonds were involved. Back when her dad was alive, the group would have only just been starting. Now, everyone knew their names.

Had they started out as loan sharks? It wouldn't surprise her. Every operation had to start somewhere. Was her dad one of their first customers perhaps?

She had to find someone from this seedy organization; the only problem was they kept themselves underground. Back in her youth, the rumors were that group members sewed blades into their boots, and that every member was branded with a diamond scar somewhere on their body. But that might have just been high school talk.

She needed to dig deeper and find them. Starting tomorrow, she was going to find this Owen Angels for herself.

Her cell phone began buzzing on her desk. She checked the screen.

INCOMING CALL: WILLIAM EDIS.

The director, probably wanting a review of the case. She sometimes wished he'd give her more time to prepare them, but she understood the urgency. The media would want the lowdown by the morning.

She picked it up. "Hi director. Me and Nigel are back. Case closed."

"Miss Dark, are you sitting down?"

Damn it, he wants me in his office already. "Yes I am. I'm at my desk. Do you want me upstairs? I can run you through the…"

"No, please," Edis interrupted. "This isn't about the case. This is something else."

"Oh, certainly. I'm all yours."

"I'll warn you in advance. You won't like what you're about to hear."

Ella's felt a sense of vertigo, like she was at the top of an impossibly high skyscraper looking over the edge. "Okay. What is it?"

"Miss Dark, Tobias Campbell escaped from prison tonight."

In her vision, she fell from the skyscraper and hurtled towards concrete at terminal velocity. Her last thoughts were a barrage of questions, the loudest of which was *how the hell is that possible?* Ella found herself unable to utter a reply. She tried to speak but some invisible force prevented her from doing so.

You didn't think I'd forgotten about you, did you?

"Ella, are you okay?"

"No."

"If you like, we can put you somewhere safe for the time being. Is that an option for you?"

I'll see you soon.

The notes were from him. They weren't some pranks or some relationship test from Mark. Tobias Campbell had eyes on her in Delaware. Her sense of vulnerability reached an all-time high. The thought of this psychopath knowing her exact whereabouts made her entire body itch.

"Miss Dark?

Ella lost herself in the white light of her computer screen. She remembered her moment with Byford in her motel room. She was calm and capable. She had weapons, fighting skills, allies. Other serial killers had fallen at her feet, and Tobias was flesh and blood just like them. If that son of a bitch wanted to fight, he was going to get one.

"No, director. I'm perfectly fine thank you."

She hung up, overflowing with questions but not quite ready to learn the answers just yet. She grabbed her bag and headed home.

CHAPTER THIRTY ONE

Ella didn't go straight home. She drove around for a while, collecting her thoughts. She'd once read that the best place to reflect was either in the car or on the toilet, and she believed it to be absolutely true. She pulled into her apartment complex around ten pm. Before exiting the car, she checked her phone for messages. Nothing from Mark; he must have given up, thank God.

But she didn't care about him anymore. There was someone else she needed to talk to. Someone who knew her problem like no one else.

Ella entered the complex and took the stairs to her apartment. She trod lightly, taking every corner and every door slowly. Tobias knew where she lived, and if she was smart, she knew she couldn't live here for the foreseeable future. If she did, she'd be constantly on edge, wondering if the noisy pipes were actually an intruder sneaking through her windows. She couldn't live like that, so she needed a new place to go. Maybe she could rent somewhere or take the director up on his offer. She'd make her decision once she'd thought it through.

Her hallway was clear. No signs of intrusion. No dead animals on her doorstep. She put her key into the door, pushed it open but remained in the hallway.

This wasn't normal.

The lights were all turned off. Jenna never turned the lights off before she left. She always blamed her forgetfulness, but the truth was she was scared of the dark. There was no way Jenna hadn't been back here in three days.

Ella instinctively reached for her pistol, knowing full well it wasn't there. She switched the hallway light on and listened for any signs of life from inside.

"Hello? Jenna?"

Then something from inside the lounge. She knew that sound. It was the sound of the boards below the sofa creaking.

Should she turn and run? Call the police? It wasn't like anyone inside could escape from a top floor apartment without her noticing.

No. These colors don't run from cold bloody war.

"You're not going anywhere," a voice called from inside.

Her insides knotted up. She knew the voice. She'd done everything she could to escape it.

She opened the door to another layer of darkness, but she saw a figure sitting on her sofa, black on black.

"Mark," she said. "What the hell?"

"Exactly. What the hell," he said, rising to his feet. He flipped the light switch beside him. The sudden light blinded Ella.

"Why are you here? How did you get in my home?"

"Your roommate is careless," he said. "So, you're in Delaware, huh?"

Ella took her bags to the adjoining kitchen and dumped them on the worktop. She couldn't believe the nerve of this guy. Watching her, keeping tabs on her. She already had one stalker to worry about, she didn't need another.

"No, I *was* in Delaware. Now I'm in Washington, D.C., okay?"

Mark stood dead center in the middle of the lounge. "You didn't think to tell me you were coming back?"

"I didn't know I was coming home until this morning."

Mark checked his watch. "Right. And it's ten pm now, so what have you been doing for twelve hours?"

"Clearing up. Talking to police. Filling out reports. Talking to the director. You know how it works. You've done it long enough."

"Yeah, I have, and not a single time did I completely ignore my partner all day. And after the conversation we had the other night? I'm suspicious," Mark slammed his palm against the wall. "I'm suspicious as hell."

The noise made her take a step back from him. "Suspicious? How many times do I have to tell you? You can't be this jealous; it's not normal. You have nothing to worry about."

Mark moved in front of the door, blocking the only exit. "Ella, I'm looking at the facts here. My girlfriend flies out to another state all on her own, with a new man by her side. And she texts her boyfriend, what, a few times over 48 hours? I'm not an idiot."

She'd had enough. This was wasted energy. She thought maybe when she saw Mark in the flesh, her feelings for him might surge back.

They didn't. She disliked him as much as she did yesterday. Ella moved over to the sofa and sat down. "Come here," she said sternly.

"I'm not coming anywhere. You need to start explaining yourself. Admit it, have you been sleeping with this new guy?"

Ella dropped her head back in her seat and sighed. "Mark, sorry, but I'm all out of shits to give." She got out of her chair and stood in front of him. "This isn't working for me. I don't want to be with you..."

Smack.

Her cheek burned red hot. The sting traveled through her jaw, up her cheek and into her eye. One side of her face went numb with pain. In the past two days, she'd seen sights no human being should ever see, but being slapped in the face by the man supposed to be her boyfriend was an even greater shock.

Mark lowered his trembling hand. His mouth fell open in a look of horror. "Oh my God. Ella, I'm sorry," he cried. "I didn't mean to do that. I didn't."

Ella said nothing. She gently felt her cheek with her hand. Her skin was scalding to the touch. Mark reached out to put his arms around her, but Ella moved back and held him at arms' length.

"Don't fucking touch me."

"Please, that was an accident. I can't control my temper. I'm seeing a therapist about it, I swear."

Ella had reached her limit. After the past few weeks, her body and mind were both worn down to the nub. Humans were not designed to be exposed to this much stress, this much tragedy. She felt like every little thing chipped away at the very core of her being until there was nothing left but an empty shell.

"Ella? I'm sorry. Can we talk?"

No, they couldn't.

Ella pushed Mark out of the way, the force burning her forearm injury. She ignored it. She didn't care anymore. Pain be damned, she could handle it.

"Don't go. We need to talk."

She pushed herself up against Mark, brought her eyes to his. She curled her fist so hard it felt like a ball of granite on the end of her wrist.

"When I get back, you better not be here."

She wasn't going to hit him back. No way would she stoop so low. Ella stormed out of the front door and didn't look back.

She had somewhere else to be.

***

Ella had never been here before, but she found the address in one of her old files. She stood out in the road, in the impenetrable country darkness, looking up at the lone house. Forbidding, unknown, silent.

The house was a grandiose piece of work. A driveway big enough for ten cars, three-stories of magnificent brick work and acres of green in every direction. It overlooked the beautiful Ozette Lake, and the nearest neighbor must have been a mile away or more.

It didn't surprise her.

Ella shuffled up the cobblestone driveway to the front door, telling herself over and over again that this needed to be done. When she reached it, she raised her hand to knock, then lowered it again.

Midnight had come and gone. Would this be better at a more appropriate hour? Or was it equally as inappropriate at any hour?

Ella smelled the homely scent of the porch, saw the coats and boots hanging up on the inside. This was someone's home, and she was invading it. Just like Mark had done, just like Tobias has done. Maybe she should learn lessons from those monsters and do everything she could to be the opposite of them?

This was wrong. She hadn't been invited.

Ella stood still for a few minutes, feeling a comfort she hadn't felt in a long time. But it was not her comfort to have. She was stealing it and she had to give it back.

She turned back down the driveway, leaving behind comfort but taking morality with her. A small victory if ever there was one.

"Dark," the voice said.

Ella stopped, stared out at the crystalline lake in the distance. How much she'd missed that simple remark. She spun back around, locking eyes with her once-partner from twenty feet away.

"Mia."

The woman at the door looked as immaculate as ever. Flowing red locks, a sculpted figure that any woman would kill for, let alone ones aged 55. The only difference was that Mia was wearing a satin gown, making it the only time Ella had seen in anything but her work clothes.

Mia walked out into the porch and flipped a switch. A blinding orange light burned down from above. After rehearsing this conversation over and over for the past two weeks, Ella found herself unable to speak. Ella knew Mia wouldn't miss a thing, either. By now she would have seen the bruise on her cheek and the soreness in her eyes.

"Have you been crying?" asked Mia.

"Yes."

172

"Why are you here?"

"Because I didn't know where else to go."

Mia stormed back towards the door, pulled it open and waited.

It was an invitation.

Ella couldn't believe it.

"I've heard the news," Mia said. "Come inside. We need to talk."

NOW AVAILABLE!

GIRL, ERASED
(An Ella Dark FBI Suspense Thriller—Book 6)

FBI Special Agent Ella Dark has studied serial killers from the time she could read, devastated by the murder of her own sister, and has gained an encyclopedic knowledge of murderers. When doctors are found murdered in brutal ways, their bodies crammed into tubes and left on display, Ella struggles to see the connection. Has her knowledge reached its match?

"A MASTERPIECE OF THRILLER AND MYSTERY. Blake Pierce did a magnificent job developing characters with a psychological side so well described that we feel inside their minds, follow their fears and cheer for their success. Full of twists, this book will keep you awake until the turn of the last page."
--Books and Movie Reviews, Roberto Mattos (re Once Gone)

GIRL, ERASED (An Ella Dark FBI Suspense Thriller) is book #6 in a long-anticipated new series by #1 bestseller and USA Today bestselling author Blake Pierce, whose bestseller Once Gone (a free download) has received over 1,000 five star reviews.

FBI Agent Ella Dark, 29, is given her big chance to achieve her life's dream: to join the Behavioral Crimes Unit. Ella's hidden obsession of gaining an encyclopedic knowledge of serial killers has led to her being singled out for her brilliant mind, and invited to join the big leagues.

But what is the common thread between these latest murders?

And can Ella figure it out and save the next victim's life?

A page-turning and harrowing crime thriller featuring a brilliant and tortured FBI agent, the ELLA DARK series is a riveting mystery, packed with suspense, twists and turns, revelations, and driven by a breakneck pace that will keep you flipping pages late into the night.

Books #7-#9 are also available!

Blake Pierce

Blake Pierce is the USA Today bestselling author of the RILEY PAGE mystery series, which includes seventeen books. Blake Pierce is also the author of the MACKENZIE WHITE mystery series, comprising fourteen books; of the AVERY BLACK mystery series, comprising six books; of the KERI LOCKE mystery series, comprising five books; of the MAKING OF RILEY PAIGE mystery series, comprising six books; of the KATE WISE mystery series, comprising seven books; of the CHLOE FINE psychological suspense mystery, comprising six books; of the JESSE HUNT psychological suspense thriller series, comprising twenty one books; of the AU PAIR psychological suspense thriller series, comprising three books; of the ZOE PRIME mystery series, comprising six books; of the ADELE SHARP mystery series, comprising fifteen books, of the EUROPEAN VOYAGE cozy mystery series, comprising four books; of the new LAURA FROST FBI suspense thriller, comprising six books (and counting); of the new ELLA DARK FBI suspense thriller, comprising eleven books (and counting); of the A YEAR IN EUROPE cozy mystery series, comprising nine books, of the AVA GOLD mystery series, comprising six books (and counting); and of the RACHEL GIFT mystery series, comprising six books (and counting).

An avid reader and lifelong fan of the mystery and thriller genres, Blake loves to hear from you, so please feel free to visit www.blakepierceauthor.com to learn more and stay in touch.

BOOKS BY BLAKE PIERCE

RACHEL GIFT MYSTERY SERIES
HER LAST WISH (Book #1)
HER LAST CHANCE (Book #2)
HER LAST HOPE (Book #3)
HER LAST FEAR (Book #4)
HER LAST CHOICE (Book #5)
HER LAST BREATH (Book #6)

AVA GOLD MYSTERY SERIES
CITY OF PREY (Book #1)
CITY OF FEAR (Book #2)
CITY OF BONES (Book #3)
CITY OF GHOSTS (Book #4)
CITY OF DEATH (Book #5)
CITY OF VICE (Book #6)

A YEAR IN EUROPE
A MURDER IN PARIS (Book #1)
DEATH IN FLORENCE (Book #2)
VENGEANCE IN VIENNA (Book #3)
A FATALITY IN SPAIN (Book #4)

ELLA DARK FBI SUSPENSE THRILLER
GIRL, ALONE (Book #1)
GIRL, TAKEN (Book #2)
GIRL, HUNTED (Book #3)
GIRL, SILENCED (Book #4)
GIRL, VANISHED (Book 5)
GIRL ERASED (Book #6)
GIRL, FORSAKEN (Book #7)
GIRL, TRAPPED (Book #8)
GIRL, EXPENDABLE (Book #9)
GIRL, ESCAPED (Book #10)
GIRL, HIS (Book #11)

LAURA FROST FBI SUSPENSE THRILLER

ALREADY GONE (Book #1)
ALREADY SEEN (Book #2)
ALREADY TRAPPED (Book #3)
ALREADY MISSING (Book #4)
ALREADY DEAD (Book #5)
ALREADY TAKEN (Book #6)

EUROPEAN VOYAGE COZY MYSTERY SERIES
MURDER (AND BAKLAVA) (Book #1)
DEATH (AND APPLE STRUDEL) (Book #2)
CRIME (AND LAGER) (Book #3)
MISFORTUNE (AND GOUDA) (Book #4)
CALAMITY (AND A DANISH) (Book #5)
MAYHEM (AND HERRING) (Book #6)

ADELE SHARP MYSTERY SERIES
LEFT TO DIE (Book #1)
LEFT TO RUN (Book #2)
LEFT TO HIDE (Book #3)
LEFT TO KILL (Book #4)
LEFT TO MURDER (Book #5)
LEFT TO ENVY (Book #6)
LEFT TO LAPSE (Book #7)
LEFT TO VANISH (Book #8)
LEFT TO HUNT (Book #9)
LEFT TO FEAR (Book #10)
LEFT TO PREY (Book #11)
LEFT TO LURE (Book #12)
LEFT TO CRAVE (Book #13)
LEFT TO LOATHE (Book #14)
LEFT TO HARM (Book #15)

THE AU PAIR SERIES
ALMOST GONE (Book#1)
ALMOST LOST (Book #2)
ALMOST DEAD (Book #3)

ZOE PRIME MYSTERY SERIES
FACE OF DEATH (Book#1)
FACE OF MURDER (Book #2)

FACE OF FEAR (Book #3)
FACE OF MADNESS (Book #4)
FACE OF FURY (Book #5)
FACE OF DARKNESS (Book #6)

A JESSIE HUNT PSYCHOLOGICAL SUSPENSE SERIES
THE PERFECT WIFE (Book #1)
THE PERFECT BLOCK (Book #2)
THE PERFECT HOUSE (Book #3)
THE PERFECT SMILE (Book #4)
THE PERFECT LIE (Book #5)
THE PERFECT LOOK (Book #6)
THE PERFECT AFFAIR (Book #7)
THE PERFECT ALIBI (Book #8)
THE PERFECT NEIGHBOR (Book #9)
THE PERFECT DISGUISE (Book #10)
THE PERFECT SECRET (Book #11)
THE PERFECT FAÇADE (Book #12)
THE PERFECT IMPRESSION (Book #13)
THE PERFECT DECEIT (Book #14)
THE PERFECT MISTRESS (Book #15)
THE PERFECT IMAGE (Book #16)
THE PERFECT VEIL (Book #17)
THE PERFECT INDISCRETION (Book #18)
THE PERFECT RUMOR (Book #19)
THE PERFECT COUPLE (Book #20)
THE PERFECT MURDER (Book #21)

CHLOE FINE PSYCHOLOGICAL SUSPENSE SERIES
NEXT DOOR (Book #1)
A NEIGHBOR'S LIE (Book #2)
CUL DE SAC (Book #3)
SILENT NEIGHBOR (Book #4)
HOMECOMING (Book #5)
TINTED WINDOWS (Book #6)

KATE WISE MYSTERY SERIES
IF SHE KNEW (Book #1)
IF SHE SAW (Book #2)
IF SHE RAN (Book #3)

IF SHE HID (Book #4)
IF SHE FLED (Book #5)
IF SHE FEARED (Book #6)
IF SHE HEARD (Book #7)

THE MAKING OF RILEY PAIGE SERIES
WATCHING (Book #1)
WAITING (Book #2)
LURING (Book #3)
TAKING (Book #4)
STALKING (Book #5)
KILLING (Book #6)

RILEY PAIGE MYSTERY SERIES
ONCE GONE (Book #1)
ONCE TAKEN (Book #2)
ONCE CRAVED (Book #3)
ONCE LURED (Book #4)
ONCE HUNTED (Book #5)
ONCE PINED (Book #6)
ONCE FORSAKEN (Book #7)
ONCE COLD (Book #8)
ONCE STALKED (Book #9)
ONCE LOST (Book #10)
ONCE BURIED (Book #11)
ONCE BOUND (Book #12)
ONCE TRAPPED (Book #13)
ONCE DORMANT (Book #14)
ONCE SHUNNED (Book #15)
ONCE MISSED (Book #16)
ONCE CHOSEN (Book #17)

MACKENZIE WHITE MYSTERY SERIES
BEFORE HE KILLS (Book #1)
BEFORE HE SEES (Book #2)
BEFORE HE COVETS (Book #3)
BEFORE HE TAKES (Book #4)
BEFORE HE NEEDS (Book #5)
BEFORE HE FEELS (Book #6)
BEFORE HE SINS (Book #7)